Thomas Percival

Moral and Literary Dissertations

Thomas Percival

Moral and Literary Dissertations

ISBN/EAN: 9783337337902

Printed in Europe, USA, Canada, Australia, Japan

Cover: Foto ©Andreas Hilbeck / pixelio.de

More available books at **www.hansebooks.com**

MORAL AND LITERARY

DISSERTATIONS;

CHIEFLY INTENDED AS THE SEQUEL

TO

A FATHER's INSTRUCTIONS.

REM TIBI SOCRATICÆ POTERUNT OSTENDERE
CHARTÆ.

————— QUO VIRTUS; QUO FERAT ERROR.

HOR.

MORAL AND LITERARY

DISSERTATIONS,

ON THE

FOLLOWING SUBJECTS;

1. On *Truth* and *Faithfulness*.
2. On *Habit* and *Association*.
3. On *Inconsistency* of *Expectation* in *Literary Pursuits*.
4. On a *Taste* for the general *Beauties* of *Nature*.
5. On a *Taste* for the *Fine Arts*.
6. On the *Alliance* of *Natural History*, and *Philosophy*, with *Poetry*.

TO WHICH ARE ADDED

A TRIBUTE TO THE MEMORY OF

CHARLES DE POLIER, ESQ.

AND AN

APPENDIX.

BY

THOMAS PERCIVAL, M.D. F.R.S. & S.A.

MEMBER OF THE MEDICAL SOCIETIES
OF LONDON AND EDINBURGH,
AND OF THE ROYAL SOCIETY OF PHYSICIANS
AT PARIS, &c. &c.

WARRINGTON,

Printed by W. EYRES, for J. JOHNSON, St. Paul's Church-Yard,

LONDON.

MDCCLXXXIV.

MY LORD,

THE approbation, with which your lordſhip has been pleaſed to honour the firſt part of the Work, now offered to your acceptance, encourages me to hope that you will receive the ſubſequent Diſſertations, with the ſame friendly and

A 3   candid

candid indulgence. And I am happy in the prefent opportunity, of publicly expreffing the refpect, efteem, and attachment with which I have the honour to be,

MY LORD,

Your Lordfhip's

much obliged,

and moft faithful

humble Servant,

THOMAS PERCIVAL.

P R E F A C E.

IN offering to the public a mif-cellaneous work, like the follow-ing, it may be proper to give a brief account of the different parts, of which it is compofed. The SOCRATIC DISCOURSE was written feveral years ago, for the ufe of the author's own family; and a few printed copies of it were diftributed amongft his friends. The appro-bation with which it has been honour-ed, by fome of the moft judicious of them, has abated his diffidence con-cerning it; and the defire of render-ing his private labours of utility to

mankind,

mankind, has induced him to commit it again to the prefs. It forms the firft part of a plan, which he has long had in contemplation, of teaching his older children the moft important branches of ethics, viz. VERACITY, FAITHFULNESS, JUSTICE, and BENEVOLENCE, in a *fyftematic* and *experimental* manner, by EXAMPLES. But various caufes have hitherto prevented, and will probably continue to prevent, the completion of his defign. He cordially wifhes, therefore, that fome moralift, of more leifure and fuperior abilities, into whofe hands this little piece may fall, would execute, in its full extent, what is here fo partially and imperfectly attempted.

To promote the love of truth, and to excite an averfion to duplicity and

falfhood;

falfhood, are objects which merit the moft ferious attention, in the bufinefs of education. And as the minds of children, at an early age, are incapable of difcerning the diftinctions and fubordinations of moral duty, the rules, prefcribed to them, fhould be abfolute and without exception. But in the more advanced period of youth, obfervation and reading will neceffarily point out many deviations from thefe rules, not only in the converfation and conduct of their friends, but in the moft applauded actions which hiftory records. And when fuch reflections fuggeft themfelves, it is a proof that the powers of the underftanding are unfolded; and that it will be feafonable to graft rational knowledge on the love of virtue. For to obviate error, is the firft ftep towards rectitude; and the abufe of reafon, in our

moral

moral judgments, too frequently terminates in depravity of principle.

The author has, in general, given his authorities for the facts, which he has related, that hiſtoric truth may be diſtinguiſhed from the fictions, introduced for the ſake of illuſtration : But in the ſtory of the king of Navarre, afterwards Henry IV. of France, they have been unavoidably intermingled. The reference to Sully's Memoirs will, however, ſhew were the former ends, and the latter commences.

It is well known to the learned, that Socrates gave riſe to a new mode of inſtruction, in the ſchools of philoſophy ; and that Plato and Xenophon, by recording the moral converſations of their amiable maſter, excited a taſte for dialogue, which

has

has prevailed through all succeeding ages. The mode of exemplification, pursued in the present work, has necessarily occasioned some deviation from each of these great originals; who are, indeed, themselves so different, as to agree only in one common outline. But he has copied both in many particulars; especially in the adoption of real characters, for the *dramatis personæ*, or speakers in his discourse. How far he has done justice to the talents or opinions of Philocles, it is not for him to determine. But if the sentiments, imputed to his late honoured friend, be such as he would not have avowed; let it be remembered, that Plato also wrote what Socrates disclaimed; * and that the author alone

is

---

* The Lysis. When Socrates heard this dialogue of Plato read, in which he supported

the

is anſwerable for whatever he has delivered.

The ESSAYS on the INFLUENCE of HABIT and ASSOCIATION; on INCONSISTENCY of EXPECTATION in LITERARY PURSUITS; on the ADVANTAGES of a TASTE for the GENERAL BEAUTIES of NATURE and of ART; and on the ALLIANCE of NATURAL HISTORY and PHILOSOPHY with POETRY, have been read before the LITERARY and PHILOSOPHICAL SOCIETY, of Mancheſter, and honoured with a place in their journals. But in theſe ſeveral compoſitions, the diſcerning reader will perceive evident traits of paternal inſtruction: And that both

the principal character, "Gods!" he exclaimed, "how this young man makes me ſay what I "never thought!"

in

in the choice of the subjects, and in the experimental method of discussing them, he has had in view, the interests of those, in whose improvement he is most nearly and tenderly concerned. They will therefore, he trusts, be deemed no improper sequel to the SOCRATIC DISCOURSE.

The composition of a TRIBUTE to the MEMORY of CHARLES DE POLIER, ESQ. devolved upon him, as the friend of the deceased, and officially as president of the very respectable society, which appointed this record of his merit. It was written under the impression of heartfelt sorrow; and on that account may, perhaps, be suspected of exhibiting a picture, too strong in its lineaments, and too glowing in its colours. But time, which calms every emotion,

and

and restores the due authority of judgment over imagination, has made no change in the author's sentiments, concerning the character he has drawn. And the insertion of it, in this work, whilst it gratifies the feelings of his mind, is perfectly consonant to the general design, which he has in view. For it offers a most instructive model to young men, who are animated with the laudable ambition of uniting liberal and polite manners, with the more solid attainments of learning and virtue.

The APPENDIX to the SOCRATIC DISCOURSE contains such remarks and illustrations, as further reflection or reading have suggested, since that piece was written. The author is fully apprized of the peculiar delicacy and difficulty of the moral topics,

which

which he has attempted to invefti-
gate ; and trufts, that he fhall always
be difpofed to acknowledge and to
rectify any errors, into which he
may have fallen. For he deems a
return to truth and reafon, more
honourable than the poffeffion even of
infallible judgment ; and fincerely
adopts the fentiment of a celebrated
writer ; " that the man, who is free
" from miftakes, can pretend to no
" praife, except what is derived from
" the juftnefs of his underftanding ;
" but that he, who corrects his mif-
" takes, difplays at once, the juftnefs
" of his underftanding, and the can-
" dour of his heart."

MANCHESTER, *September* 1, 1783.

Page 62, line 15, for Shakefpear, *read* Shakefpeare.
   92,   6,   authorifed, *read* authorized.
   98,   7,   *id.*   *id.*
  100,   13,   apologifed, *read* apologized.
  107,   14,   philofophifing, *read* philofophizing.
  110,   18,   Chimæras, *read* Chimeras.
  145,   Note,   Shakefpear's, *read* Shakefpeare's.
  147,   3,   characterifed, *read* characterized.
  209,   23,   humanifes, *read* humanizes.
  212,   14,   civilifed, *read* civilized.
  248,   8,   lightenings, *read* lightnings.
  ——   19,   *id.*   *id.*
  249,   3,   Shakefpear, *read* Shakefpeare.
  319,   16,   authorifed, *read* authorized.

N. B. The Author having fuppreffed feveral fections, intended for infertion in the Appendix, the references in the Socratic Difcourfe, to pages 19, 20, 53, 76, 85, 102, 108, are confequently erroneous.

TABLE

OF

CONTENTS.

APPENDIX.

A

SOCRATIC DISCOURSE

ON

TRUTH.

INTER SILVAS ACADEMI QUÆRERE
VERUM.

HOR.

A

SOCRATIC DISCOURSE

ON

T R U T H.

———————

TO

T. B. P.

YOU have often been a witnefs, my dear Son, of the pleafure experienced by me, in the recollection of the Academical years, which I paffed at ——— in the purfuit of general fcience, before I engaged in my profeffional ftudies at the univerfity of ———. And you have no lefs frequently heard me exprefs the higheft

B 2

veneration

veneration for the profound learning, and exalted character of Philocles, under whose tuition, the charms of knowledge first attracted my regard. I have lately revisited those scenes so delightful to my youth: But, leaving to your conception the emotions which I felt, I shall relate to you a SOCRATIC CONVERSATION, that occurred there in my presence, between Philocles and your kinsman Sophron. This amiable youth, who is likely to reflect a lustre on the sacred office, to which, I trust, he will ere long be called, had been reciting to his Professor an Academical composition on the importance of TRUTH, and on the folly, infamy, and baseness of LYING and DECEIT. And, when he laid down the book, Philocles expressed an earnest wish, that such sentiments might ever influence the heart, and direct the conduct of his pupil. But general rules, continued he, are insufficient for our government in the diversified and complicated occurrences

of

of life: And, if we be ambitious of acting with wisdom, honour, and virtue, it is neceſſary that we ſhould make ourſelves acquainted with the various branches and ſubordinations of each moral duty. Let us, therefore, take a particular view of TRUTH, and of her inſeparable companion FAITHFULNESS. You are no novice in theſe ſubjects; and Euphronius, I am perſuaded, will be pleaſed to hear you exerciſed in the diſcuſſion of them.

I preſume you will concur with me in opinion, that MORAL TRUTH is the *conformity of our expreſſions to our thoughts*; and FAITHFULNESS, *that of our actions to our expreſſions:* And that LYING or FALSHOOD *is generally a mean, ſelfiſh, or malevolent, and always an unjuſtifiable endeavour to deceive another, by ſignifying or aſſerting that to be truth or fact, which is known or believed to be otherwiſe; and by making promiſes, without any intention to perform them.*

B 3

But,

But, if we believe our affertions or figns to be true, and they fhould afterwards prove to be falfe, tell me, Sophron, are we then guilty of Lying?

No, replied Sophron; we fhall have committed only an error or miftake: For under fuch circumftances, we muft have been deceived ourfelves; and could have had no defign of impofing upon others.

But is every breach of promife a Lie, continued Philocles?

I fhould think not, anfwered Sophron, if the promife were made with fincerity, and the violation of it be unavoidable.

Your diftinction is juft, faid Philocles; and there are alfo certain conditions, obvious to the general fenfe of mankind, underftood or implied in almoft every promife, on which the performance muft depend. Whang-to, Emperor of China,

who

who governed his people like a father, and regarded his own elevation and power as trusts delegated for their good, had a daughter who was his only child, and the darling of his old age. He promised her in marriage to Oufan-quey, the son of his favourite mandarine, and that he would bequeath to him all his dominions as her dowry. Oufan-quey was at that time a youth of the most promising abilities and difpofitions; but the profpect of royalty, and the adulation of a court, foon corrupted his heart. He became haughty, infolent, and cruel; and the people anticipated, with horror, the tyranny which they muft endure under his government. By the inftitutions of the Chinefe, the great officers of ftate may remonftrate to the emperor, when his decrees are injurious to the public intereft; and this privilege has often tended to abate the rigour of defpotifm. Whang-to heard, with grief and aftonifhment, the complaints

of

of his mandarines againſt Ouſan-quey.
He ſummoned him into his preſence, and
being ſatisfied with the proofs of his
demerit, he addreſſed the officers of ſtate
in the following terms : " I engaged
" my daughter in marriage, and pro-
" miſed the inheritance of my dominions
" to Ouſan-quey, a youth who was wiſe,
" humane, and juſt. In departing from
" virtue, he has cancelled theſe obliga-
" tions, and forfeited his title to both."
Then turning to Ouſan-quey, he ſaid,
" I command you to retire from 'my
" court, and to paſs the remainder of
" your days in the moſt diſtant province
" of my empire."

But is it not deemed peculiarly honourable, Sophron, to perform a promiſe, when paſſion or ſelf-intereſt ſtrongly
incites us to the violation of it ?

Nothing raiſes our admiration higher,
ſaid Sophron ; and I beg leave to relate

to

to you a story, which places this truth in a very striking point of view. A Spanish cavalier, without any reasonable provocation, assassinated a Moorish gentleman, and instantly fled from justice. He was vigorously pursued; but availing himself of a sudden turn in the road, he leaped, unperceived, over a garden wall. The proprietor, who was also a Moor, happened to be, at that time, walking in the garden; and the Spaniard fell upon his knees before him, acquainted him with his case, and in the most pathetic manner, implored concealment. The Moor listened to him with compassion, and generously promised his assistance. He then locked him in a summer-house, and left him, with an assurance that, when night approached, he would provide for his escape. A few hours afterwards, the dead body of his son was brought to him; and the description of the murderer exactly agreed with the appearance of

the

the Spaniard, whom he had then in cuftody. He concealed the horror and fufpicion which he felt; and retiring to his chamber, remained there till midnight. Then, going privately into the garden, he opened the door of the fummer-houfe, and thus accofted the cavalier: "Chriftian," faid he, "the youth "whom you have murdered was my "only fon. Your crime merits the fe- "vereft punifhment. But I have fo- "lemnly pledged my word for your "fecurity; and I difdain to violate even "a rafh engagement with a cruel ene- "my." He conducted the Spaniard to the ftables, and furnifhing him with one of his fwifteft mules, "Fly," faid he, "whilft the darknefs of the night con- "ceals you. Your hands are polluted "with blood; but GOD is juft; and I "humbly thank him that my faith is "unfpotted, and that I have refigned "judgment unto him."*

* See Hiftor. Mirror.

When,

When Sophron had finished this narrative, I took the liberty of observing that Faithfulness is a virtue, which we sometimes meet with in very abandoned characters, who are neither influenced by a sense of religious, nor of moral obligation. In such persons it is founded on certain ideas of HONOUR, which originally spring from the best natural principles.* After the battle of Culloden, in the year 1745, a reward of thirty thousand pounds was offered to any one, who should discover or deliver up the young Pretender. He had taken refuge with the Kennedies, two common thieves; who protected him with fidelity; robbed for his support; and often went in disguise to Inverness, to buy provisions for him. A considerable time afterwards, one of these men, who had resisted the temptation of thirty thousand pounds, was hanged for stealing a cow, of the value of thirty shillings.†

* Vid. Appendix, Sect. I.   † See Pennant's Tour in Scotland.

But

But I apprehend, refumed Sophron, with much modefty, that there are cafes in which it would be more culpable to fulfil, than to violate a promife.

To this propofition Philocles gave his full affent, and illuftrated it by the following fuppofititious cafe. A brace of loaded piftols have been left in my hands by a friend, to whom I have engaged to reftore them, whenever he fhall make the demand. But if he claim them when intoxicated with liquor, or mad with paffion and refentment, it is evident that the performance of my promife would not only be weak, but extremely reprehenfible: And my friend himfelf, in his calm and fober moments, would be amongft the firft to charge me with all the mifchiefs, occafioned by my erroneous fenfe of duty. Hafty declarations and rafh affeverations are fometimes made by good men, who cannot however reafonably or confcien-

tioufly

tiouſly fulfil them. When Jeſus had waſhed the feet of ſeveral of his diſciples, he came to Simon Peter: "*And* "*Peter ſaid unto him, Lord, doſt thou* "*waſh my feet? Jeſus anſwered and ſaid,* "*What I do, thou knoweſt not now; but* "*thou ſhalt know hereafter. Peter ſaid unto* "*him, Thou ſhalt never waſh my feet!* "*Jeſus anſwered him, If I waſh thee not,* "*thou haſt no part with me. Simon Peter* "*ſaid unto him, Lord, not my feet only,* "*but alſo my hands and my head.*"* Nor can even vows, however ſolemn, be binding, when the object of them is the commiſſion of a crime. For though appeals to the Deity are ſacred pledges of our ſincerity, they make no change in the nature or legality of actions. And it would be the groſſeſt ſuperſtition to ſuppoſe, that the violation of God's ordinances can either be honourable, or acceptable to him.† David, in revenge for an inſult offered him

* John, Chap. xiii.　　† See Appendix, Sect II.

by

by Nabal, vowed that he would put to the ſword every male of his family. But his wrath was afterwards appeaſed; and he became ſo ſenſible of the injuſtice of his deſign, that he ſaid, *" Bleſſed " be the* LORD, *who has kept his ſervant " from evil."**

It ſhould ſeem, that the Roman emperor Trajan thought it might be criminal in his officers, under certain circumſtances, to maintain the allegiance which they had ſworn to him.† On the appointment of Suberanus to be captain of the royal guard, he preſented him with a ſword, as the badge of his fealty, ſaying, " Let this be drawn in " my defence, if I rule according to " equity; but if otherwiſe, it may be " employed againſt me." ‡

* 1 Sam. xxv. 22.

† See Appendix, Sect. III.   ‡ Plin.

The

The conclusion concerning the observance of promises, may be extended to Veracity, notwithstanding the extravagant declaration of one of the Fathers, " that he would not violate truth, though " he were sure to gain heaven by it." Whenever, from the concurrence of extraordinary circumstances, the practice of one virtue is rendered incompatible with the performance of another, of much higher obligation, it is evident that the inferior must yield to the superior duty. An example will elucidate, and evince the justness of this observation.

After the horrid massacre of the Huguenots in France, which began on St. Bartholomew's day, 1572, the king of Navarre was very rigorously guarded, by the order of the queen-mother, Catharine de Medicis. But one day, when he was hunting near Senlis, during the heat of the chace, he seized a favourable

opportunity

opportunity of making his efcape; and galloping through the woods, with a few faithful friends, amongft whom was young Rofny, afterwards duke of Sully, he croffed the Seine at Poiffy,* and fled to the caftle of a nobleman, who was a zealous, though fecret proteftant, and ftrongly attached to his intereft. Troops of horfe were foon difpatched, different ways, in purfuit of him. One of thefe detachments ftopped at the gates of the caftle, where Henry was then refrefhing himfelf; and the captain demanded permiffion to fearch for him, fhewing the royal mandate to bring the head of Henry, and to put his attendants to the fword. Refiftance was evidently vain; and compliance would have been a breach of hofpitality, friendfhip, and humanity; at the fame time that it muft have proved fatal to the interefts of the reformed religion, and to the whole body of proteftants

---

* See Sully's Memoirs; and alfo the Preface to this work.

in France, who had no other protector but the king of Navarre. The nobleman, therefore, without hesitation, and with an undaunted countenance, instantly said, " Waste not your time, Sir, " in fruitless searches. The king of " Navarre, with his friends, passed this " way about two hours ago; and if you " set spurs to your horse, you will over- " take him before the night approaches." The captain and his troop, satisfied with this answer, rode off at full speed; and the king was then left at liberty to provide for his safety, by disguising himself, and taking a different rout.

Under such circumstances, as you have described, all mankind, observed Sophron, would condemn a strict adherence to TRUTH.* But what do you think

* *Infani fapiens nomen ferat, æquus iniqui*
Ultra quam fatis eft, virtutem fi petat ipfam.
Hor. Ep. VI. Lib. I. V. 15.

That

think of the conduct of the Portuguese
flave, whose breach of veracity, and even
perjury, is extolled by Abbé Raynal,
in his Hiftory of the European Settle-
ments. This negro, who had fled into
the woods to enjoy the liberty which
was his natural right, having learned
that his old mafter was arrefted, and
likely to be condemned for a capital

That which being done admits of a rational juftification,
is the effence, or general character, of a MORAL DUTY.
DIALOGUE CONCERNING HAPPINESS, by JAMES HARRIS,
Efq. p. 175.

The right to truth may be forfeited in particular cafes,
as by one who hath formed a defign to kill another, and, if
not hindered, will probably accomplifh his wicked purpofe.
Neither the perfon whofe life is aimed at, fhould he fave himfelf by a lie, nor any one who fhould tell an officious lie for
him, will be guilty of the leaft injuftice to him, whom, by
this means, they keep from perpetrating the mifchief intended.
Inftead of a wrong, it is a kindnefs. GROVE'S MORAL PHI-
LOSOPHY, Vol. II. p. 415.

Adhering to the *ordinary* rules of duty, in thefe *extraordinary*
cafes, may fometimes occafion greater evils to our country,
or to mankind, than all the virtues, any one mortal can
exert, will repair. HUTCHESON'S MORAL PHILOSOPHY,
Vol. II. 4to. p 117. See a farther difcuffion of this fubject,
in the Appendix, Sect. IV. Confult alfo Genefis, Chap. xii.

crime,

crime, came into the court of juſtice; aſſumed the guilt of the fact; ſuffered himſelf to be impriſoned; brought falſe, though judicial proofs of his crime; and was executed inſtead of his beloved maſter.

The diſapprobation of falſhood, in this inſtance, anſwered Philocles, is ſuppreſſed for a while, by our admiration of the affection, gratitude, generoſity, and greatneſs of mind diſplayed by the negro. We lament the bondage of ſuch a hero; and regret that his exalted virtues were not diſplayed on a more important and honourable occaſion. But when theſe firſt emotions are over, and we diſpaſſionately reflect on the conduct of the ſlave, we muſt condemn it as an unjuſtifiable ſacrifice of truth, of his own life, and of the duty which he owed to ſociety.* The divine command, " *Thou* " *ſhalt not bear falſe witneſs* AGAINST *thy*

* See Appendix, Sect. V.

 " *neighbour,*"

" *neighbour*," cannot furely be fuppofed to imply, that he may bear *falfe witnefs in his* FAVOUR; becaufe this would be to forbid private injury, and to authorife public wrongs. Judicial teftimony, in the prefent circumftances of the moral world, is effential to the well-being of fociety; and to leffen the general credibility of it, by introducing into courts of law falfhood and perjury, is a high crime againft the ftate, and feverely punifhed in all countries which have emerged from barbarifm.* Befides, the good of the community requires that juftice fhould be executed on the offender himfelf, to prevent him from committing other crimes: And it would give encouragement to vice, if an innocent perfon, perhaps tired of life, or influenced by enthufiaftic notions of honour, friendfhip, or love, might fuffer for another who is guilty.

* See Appendix, Sect. VI.

The

The certainty of punishment, even in misdemeanors, is strongly urged by the Marquis de Beccaria, the great advocate for judicial lenity. And he thinks the forgiveness of the injured party himself, should not interrupt the execution of justice. "This may be an act of good-"nature and humanity," he observes, "but it is contrary to the good of the "public. For although a private citi-"zen may dispense with satisfaction for "his private injury, he cannot remove "the necessity of public example. The "right of punishing belongs not to any "individual in particular, but to the "society in general, or the sovereign "who represents that society: And a "man may renounce his own portion of "this right, but he cannot give up that "of others."

The conduct of the negro, said So-phron, however erroneous it might be in point of wisdom, or unjustifiable with

C 3

respect

refpect to its morality, was perfectly generous and difintereſted.   But the fame
elegant writer, who records this fact, has
related another example of the violation of truth, from motives purely *felfifh*,
which I cannot condemn, though I know
not how to juſtify.   I will endeavour to
recollect, and to repeat the ſtory.   A
Britiſh ſerjeant was taken priſoner by the
favages in America; who prepared themfelves to put him to death, with all the
barbarity which their ſkill in torture
could invent.   Shocked with the view of
the horrid fufferings which awaited him,
he thus addreffed the Indians: " Mighty
" warriors, your preparations are vain,
" for my body is invulnerable; and if
" you will fet me at liberty, I will teach
" you how to become fo.   Think not
" that I impofe upon you by falfe pre-
" tenfions.   I am willing that you fhould
" try upon me an experiment, which
" may fatisfy your doubts. Let the chief,
                                    " who

"who holds my hanger, now strike with
"all his force. I equally defy the sharp-
"ness of the instrument, and the strength
"of his arm." Whilst he was saying
these words, he bent his head, and laid
bare his neck. The Indian eagerly advanced; and by one furious blow, severed
the head from the body. Thus the poor
serjeant, by his presence of mind, exchanged lingering tortures for an easy
and instantaneous death.

Euphronius here remarked, that the
story is of doubtful authority, by the
confession of the Abbé himself. But ad-
mitting the truth of it, continued he, for
the sake of argument, what moralist can
be so rigid as not to deem the conduct
of the serjeant at least excusable? Perhaps no man, in similar circumstances,
would have acted differently, if he pos-
sessed sufficient composure to devise, or
address to practise such an expedient,
The case is not analogous to that of

martyr-

martyrdom for religion.   The horrid
fufferings to be endured, in this inftance,
could anfwer no good end ; and fociety
received not the leaft injury, either immediate or remote, by the evafion of
them.

Recollecting an hiftorical fact of un-
queftionable truth, and ftrictly applicable
to the point in debate, I requefted permiffion to relate it.   When Columbus
and his crew were caft away on an ifland,
more than thirty leagues from Hifpaniola,
nothing remained to them in profpect,
but to end their miferable days with
naked favages, far from their country
and their friends.   To add to thefe ca-
lamities, the natives began foon to mur-
mur at the refidence of the Spaniards
amongft them ;   the fupport of whom
became burthenfome to men, ignorant of
agriculture, and unaccuftomed to exertion
or induftry : They brought in provifions
with reluctance, furnifhed them fparingly,

and

and even threatened entirely to withhold them. Such a refolution muft have occafioned inevitable deftruction to the Spaniards; but Columbus prevented it by a happy device, that revived all the admiration and reverence, with which the Indians firft regarded thefe ftrangers. By his fkill in aftronomy, he knew there was fhortly to be a total eclipfe of the moon. On the day before it happened, he affembled the principal perfons of the diftrict, and after reproaching them for their defection from thofe, whom they had lately revered, he told them that the Spaniards were fervants of the Great Spirit, who dwells in heaven: That, offended at their refufal to fupport the objects of his peculiar favour, the Deity was preparing to punifh their crime with exemplary feverity; and that the moon fhould be darkened that very night, and affume a bloody hue, as a fign of the Divine wrath, and an emblem of the vengeance ready to fall on them. To
this

this marvellous prediction, fome of the barbarians liftened with carelefs indifference; others, with credulous aftonifhment : But when the moon began gradually to withdraw her light, and at length appeared of a red colour, all were ftruck with terror. They ran with confternation to their houfes, and returning to Columbus loaded with provifions, threw them inftantly at his feet, conjuring him to intercede with the Great Spirit, to avert the deftruction with which they were threatened. Columbus, feeming to be moved by their intreaties, promifed to comply with their defire. The eclipfe went off, the moon recovered its fplendour ; and from that time, the Spaniards were not only furnifhed profufely with provifions, but treated with the moft fuperftitious attention.* This folemn deceit of Columbus may be juftified by the rights of neceffity. Shipwrecked on a diftant coaft, in the profe-

* See Robertfon's Hift. of America, Vol. I. Book 2.

cution

cution of an enterprize, which, in his mind, appears to have originated from honourable and useful views, and destitute of every means of supplying himself and his associates with sustenance, he had a claim to the protection, assistance, and support of the people who were spectators of his calamity. And it was a happy fertility of genius, which suggested to him an expedient, far preferable to the force of arms. But I feel a secret wish, that this truly great man had mixed less of falsity with his artifice. He might have reprehended the Indians for their want of hospitality, alarmed their fears by his prediction, and excited their wonder and reverence by its fulfilment, without denouncing, in such unguarded terms, the immediate vengeance of Heaven. Truth is so important, and of so delicate a nature, that every possible precaution should be employed to extenuate its violation, although the sacrifice be made to duties which supersede its obligation.

Philocles

Philocles very obligingly thanked me for recalling to his memory so pertinent a fact. He then turned to his pupil, and asked him what he thought of the maxim, which some persons have adopted, " that " faith is not to be kept with rogues " or traitors ? "

I think the maxim, replied Sophron, false in itself, and highly injurious to society. For, independent of the licentiousnefs and cruelty, to which it might give rise, a man owes to his own honour and peace of mind, except on very extraordinary occasions, the strict performance of his promise. And this opinion seems to have influenced the conduct of the great Viscount Turenne, and of Sir Richard Herbert. The former was attacked one night by robbers near Paris, who stripped him of his money, watch, and rings. He engaged to give them a hundred *louis d'ors*, if they would return him a ring, of little intrinsic worth,

but

but on which he fet a particular value. The highwaymen complied; and one of them had the boldnefs to go to his houfe the fucceeding day, and in the midft of a large company to demand, in a whifper, the performance of his promife. The Vifcount gave orders for the money to be paid; and fuffered the villain to efcape, before he related the adventure.*

Sir Richard Herbert, being fent by Edward the Fourth, to reduce certain rebels in North Wales, laid fiege to Harlech caftle, in Merionethfhire; a fortrefs fo ftrong, that he defpaired of taking it but by blockade and famine. The captain of it offered to furrender, on condition that Sir Richard *would do what he could to fave his life*. The condition was accepted; and Sir Richard brought the commander to the king, requefting his majefty to grant him a pardon, as the expectation of this favour

* See Ramfay's Life of Turenne.

had

had induced him to yield up an important caſtle, which he might have de-
fended. Edward replied to Sir Richard
Herbert, " That as he had no power,
" by his commiſſion, to pardon any one,
" he might therefore, after the repre-
" ſentation hereof to his ſovereign, de-
" liver him up to juſtice." Sir Richard
Herbert anſwered, " He had not yet
" done *the beſt he could for him*; and
" therefore moſt humbly deſired his
" highneſs to do one of two things;
" either to put him again in the caſtle
" where he had been, and command
" ſome other to take him out; or, if
" his highneſs would not do ſo, to take
" his life for the captain's, that being
" the laſt proof he could give, that he
" had uſed his utmoſt endeavour to
" fulfil his promiſe." The king, finding himſelf ſo much urged, pardoned
the captain, but beſtowed on Sir Richard
Herbert no other reward for his ſervice.*

* See the Life of Lord Herbert of Cherbury.

Theſe

Thefe gentlemen, faid Philocles, difplayed a delicate fenfe of honour; and,
though I am dubious, whether the conduct of Monfieur Turenne has the fanction of the great Roman cafuift, * yet,
according to my judgment, both he and
Sir Richard Herbert acted conformably
to the laws of reafon and rectitude.   For
every *lawful* promife, made by one pof-
feffing prefence of mind, and the free
ufe of reafon, no event or confideration
fucceeding, which an unbiaffed underftanding would deem fufficient to render
it *unlawful,* ought to be religioufly obferved.†   But promifes, extorted by
fear, and that clearly contravene our
duty to fociety, are void in themfelves:
Thus an engagement made with fincerity, under the ftrong impreffions of
terror, to a highwayman or murderer,

* *Si prædonibus pactum pro capite pretium non attuleris, nulla fraus eft, ne fi juratus quidem id non feceris.* Cic. de Off. Lib. III. Cap. 29.

† See Grove's Mor. Philofophy.

not

not to bear teſtimony againſt him, can be of no validity; becauſe there ſubſiſts an antecedent claim of the community, which cannot be diſpenſed with by any of its members. I have ſuppoſed the engagement to be ſincere; for, if entered into with a previous deſign of violation, a breach of truth and faithfulneſs is in ſome degree committed, notwithſtanding its injuſtice or illegality.

But when you deliver to another as a certain truth, what you believe to be falſe, are you guilty of lying, ſhould it afterwards prove to be true?

Yes, anſwered Sophron; becauſe my intention is to deceive, and to make a ſuppoſed falſhood paſs for truth. Chian-fu was an officer in the guards of the emperor of Japan. He had formed a tender connection with one of the ladies of the court, and was on the point of marriage, when a formidable

inſurrection,

infurrection, in a diftant ifland of the empire, occafioned by the tyranny and cruel exactions of the government, obliged him to leave the capital without delay, to affume his poft in the royal army. The war was protracted through various caufes; and he bore with great impatience fo long an abfence from his miftrefs. By the influence of a bribe, he obtained permiffion from the commander in chief to return to Jeddo, for a few weeks; during which time he hoped to celebrate his nuptials. But dreading left the emperor fhould refent his defertion of the army, at fo critical a conjuncture, he pretended that he brought tidings, from the general, of an important advantage, gained over the enemy; which was likely foon to be fucceeded by a complete victory. Thefe accounts were founded on probability, not on truth. His falfhoods, however, procured him the moft favourable reception at court. He married the lady; and

after

after a week spent in festivity, prepared for his departure to join the army. An express at this time arrived, with the news of the entire defeat of the insurgents; but no mention was made of any previous dispatches by Chian-fu. The emperor suspected that he had been guilty of deceit. He was strictly examined; confessed his crime, and the motives of it; and was condemned to suffer immediate death. For lying is a capital offence, by the laws of Japan.

If truth, resumed Philocles, be an agreement between our words and thoughts, are you under an obligation to express all your thoughts?

No, said Sophron, prudence often forbids it; and it is no violation of truth to conceal those thoughts, or that knowledge, with which another has no right to be acquainted. On a particular occasion, the Jews demanded of

Jesus,

Jefus, " *What fign fheweft thou unto us?*
" *Jefus anfwered and faid, Deftroy this tem-*
" *ple, and in three days I will raife it up.*
" *Then faid the Jews, Forty and fix years*
" *was this temple in building, and wilt thou*
" *rear it up in three days? But he fpake of*
" *the temple of his body. When therefore he*
" *was arifen from the dead, his difciples*
" *remembered that he had faid this unto*
" *them.*" *

Sometimes, when improper or treacherous queftions áre afked, filence
would be no lefs dangerous, than an
explicit declaration of our fentiments.
In thefe cafes, we fhall be juftified in
the ufe of fuch evafions, as do not contradict the truth. When the chief priefts
and fcribes inquired of our Saviour,
whether it was lawful to pay tribute
unto Cæfar? " *He perceived their crafti-*
" *nefs, and faid unto them, Why tempt ye*
" *me? Shew me a penny: Whofe image*

* John, Chap. ii. Ver. 18.

" *and*

" and superscription hath it? They answered
" and said, Cæsar's. And he said unto them,
" Render unto Cæsar the things which be
" Cæsar's, and unto GOD the things which
" be GOD's. And they could not take hold
" of his words before the people: And they
" marvelled at his answers, and held their
" peace."

Under the reign of the cruel and bigoted queen Mary, the princess Elizabeth, her sister, suffered a variety of persecutions, on account of her steady attachment to the protestant religion. It is said, she was one day interrogated concerning the Lord's Supper; and that she returned the following prudent, and evasive answer:

" Christ was the word that spake it;
" He took the bread and brake it;
" And what the word did make it,
" That I believe and take it." *

* Walpole's Cat. of Royal and Noble Authors.

Philocles

Philocles expreffed much fatisfaction in the judicious diftinction, which his pupil had made, and obferved, that the conduct of the princefs Elizabeth is fully juftified by the example of the apoftle Paul, in circumftances not very diffimilar. The Athenians had a law, which rendered it capital to promulgate any new divinities.* And when Paul preached to them JESUS and the RESURRECTION, he was accufed of having broken this law, and of being a "*fetter forth of ftrange Gods*;" and was carried before the Areopagus, a court of judicature, which took cognifance of all criminal matters, and was, in a particular manner, charged with the care of the eftablifhed religion. An impoftor, in fuch a fituation, would have retracted his doctrine to fave his life; and an enthufiaft would have facrificed his life, without attempting to fave it by innocent means. But the Apoftle wifely avoided

* Socrates fuffered under this law.

 both

both extremes; and availing himſelf of an inſcription "TO THE UNKNOWN GOD," which he had ſeen upon an altar in the city, he pleaded in his own defence, "*Whom ye ignorantly worſhip, him declare I unto you.*" By this preſence of mind, he evaded the law, and eſcaped condemnation, without departing from the truth of the Goſpel, or violating the honour of GOD.*

Though I am no general admirer, continued Philocles, of the maxims of morality delivered by Lord Cheſterfield, yet I think his remarks on the preſent ſubject peculiarly worthy of attention. "The prudence and neceſſity," ſays the noble author, "of frequently concealing "the truth, inſenſibly ſeduces people to "violate it. It is the only art of mean "capacities, and the only refuge of mean "ſpirits. Whereas concealing the truth,

* Vid. Acts xvii. 23. Alſo Lord Lyttelton's Obſervations on the Converſion and Apoſtleſhip of St. Paul.

"upon

" upon proper occafions, is as prudent
" and as innocent, as telling a lie, upon
" any occafion, is infamous and foolifh.
" I will ftate you a cafe in your own
" department. Suppofe you are em-
" ployed at a foreign court, and that
" the minifter of that court is abfurd or
" impertinent enough to afk you, what
" your inftructions are; will you tell
" him a lie, which as foon as found out,
" and found out it certainly will be,
" muft deftroy your credit, blaft your
" character, and render you ufelefs there?
" No. Will you tell him the truth then,
" and betray your truft? As certainly,
" No. But you will anfwer, with firm-
" nefs, That you are furprifed at fuch
" a queftion; that you are perfuaded he
" does not expect an anfwer to it; but
" that at all events he certainly will not
" have one. Such an anfwer will give
" him confidence in you; he will con-
" ceive an opinion of your veracity, of
" which opinion you may afterwards
" make very honeft and fair advantages."
D 4　　　　Philocles

Philocles proceeded to interrogate his pupil, whether falfity, when in jeft, is to be deemed a lie? But Sophron declined the queftion, as too nice for his decifion; and defired to hear the fentiments of Philocles, who delivered them in the following terms. Wit and irony, raillery and humour, are often deviations from the ftrict rules of veracity: But they are allowed by common confent; and, under proper reftrictions, they contribute to enliven converfation, and to improve our manners. But jocularity is certainly culpable, and may be deemed a fpecies of lying, when it is intended to deceive, without any good end in view; and efpecially with the ungenerous one of diverting ourfelves at the painful expence of another. The practice alfo may lead to more criminal falfhoods; and it is related with honour of Ariftides, that he held truth to be fo facred, *ut ne joco quidem mentiretur.*

Some

Some jocular lies have produced the most serious and affecting consequences; of which I will give you an example or two, in the youthful frolics of Hilario, a nobleman who now looks back, with sorrow and regret, on the sufferings occasioned by his levity. When he was a student at Cambridge, he went at midnight crying *fire, fire!* to the chamber door of one of the fellows of ————, a gentleman universally admired for his literary and poetical abilities, but who was of a timid and melancholy disposition. The gentleman awaked out of a sound sleep, and, attentive only to the first suggestions of fear, leaped through the window, at the hazard of losing his life by the fall. Not long after this transaction, Hilario went up to London; and dining in a mixed company of persons of fashion, he happened to sit near a grave old gentleman, who took the first opportunity of making particular inquiries concerning a youth, then at

Cambridge,

Cambridge, whom he knew to be intimately acquainted with this nobleman. Hilario inftantly fufpected, that the ferious Don was a rich uncle of his friend; and determined that he would give fuch an account of the nephew, as fhould occafion a folemn letter of reproof, over which he hoped to regale himfelf, on his return to college. He therefore jocularly faid, that his companion was a fine jolly fellow, always forming connections with the girls; that he loved to rattle the dice; and that he had lately loft his next quarter's allowance, which would lower his courage at play, for fome time to come. From the alteration which he perceived in the ftranger's countenance, he was affured of the fuccefs of his *hum*, an abfurd term given to this fhameful kind of lie: And, when he got back to Cambridge, he haftened to the apartment of his friend, to enjoy the laughter which he fhould raife at his expence. But how was he fhocked

to

to find him in the delirium of a fever, occaſioned by a billet, which had been delivered the preceding day, purporting, " That Lucinda had juſt beſtowed her " hand, upon a perſon much more de- " ſerving of her affections, than he had " been repreſented to her father by Hi- " lario, his aſſociate in pleaſure, extrava- " gance, and profligacy."

By ſuch thoughtleſs, and unjuſtifiable violations of truth, Hilario was often wounding his own peace of mind, and involving his connections in diſtreſs. He was, however, at length compelled to correct this criminal habit, through the horror which he felt, on having given riſe to a fatal duel between two brothers, by jocularly inſinuating to one of them, that he was rivalled in the affections of his miſtreſs, by the other.

It would be happy, ſaid I, if we could aſcertain the reſtrictions, under which

theſe

thefe fallies of frolic and jocularity may be indulged with innocence. One general rule may, I think, be admitted, that the entertainment, which we thus create to ourfelves, fhould be fuch only as will be a future fubject of mirth even to thofe, who are the prefent fufferers by it. But, to ufe the words of an excellent moralift, " as every action may " produce effects, over which human " power has no influence, and which " human fagacity cannot forefee; we " fhould not lightly venture to the verge " of evil; nor ftrike at others, though " with a reed, left, like the rod of Mofes, " it become a ferpent in our hands."*

Philocles now purfued the fubject, by inquiring into the nature of EQUIVOCATION; which Sophron defined to be a mean expedient to avoid the declaration of truth, without verbally telling a lie. An equivocation, faid he, confifts of

* Dr. Hawkfworth.

fuch

fuch expreffions, as admit of more than one meaning. The fpeaker ufes them in one fenfe, and defigns that the hearer fhould underftand them in another. Cicero mentions a certain perfon, who made a truce with the enemy for thirty days, and treacheroufly evaded his agreement, by laying wafte the country during the nights; alledging, that the truce was for fo many *days*, not nights.* Such an equivocation as this, has all the guilt, and infamy of a lie; but I do not feel myfelf inclined to condemn the duplicity, practifed by a gentleman, on the following occafion. He was returning home from the affizes at York, and was attacked on the road by a highwayman, to whom he delivered a fmall purfe of money. The robber told him, that he fhould not be fatisfied with a few guineas; and fternly demanded the fum, which he knew he had received, and then carried about him. The

* Vid. Cicero de Officiis, Lib. I. Cap. 13.

gentleman,

gentleman, with great apparent terror, drew out of his pocket a leathern bag, and giving it to the highwayman, said, " *Take what you want*, but spare my life." The robber eagerly received it, and was tranfported with the value of his acquifition. He rode off with it, through bye lanes, till he arrived at a place of fecurity. There he ftopped to examine his booty, which to his aftonifhment he found to confift only of a quantity of halfpence, together with a copy of the dying fpeech and earneft exhortations of a malefactor, who had been executed the preceding day for robbery.

Can you acquit me, Philocles, faid I, of the criminality of equivocation, when, in the exercife of my profeffional duties, I ftudy, by cheerful looks and ambiguous words, to remove from my patients the horrors of defpair, to mitigate the apprehenfions of danger, and to deceive them into hope; that, by adminiftering

a cordial

a cordial to the drooping fpirit, I may fmooth the bed of death, or revive even expiring life? For there are maladies, which rob the Philofopher of fortitude, and the Chriftian of confolation.

From my heart I acquit you, anfwered Philocles, with his wonted humanity. You do a kindnefs, not a wrong, to the perfon whom you thus deceive; and may reafonably prefuppofe his future approbation of that conduct, which meets with the prefent acquiefcence of all his friends. The amiable and elegant Pliny, who had the niceft fenfe of honour, recites with applaufe, in a letter to Nepos, a ftory, which may perhaps contribute to fatisfy your mind, and remove your fcruples.

The hufband of the celebrated Arria, Cæcinna Pætus, was very dangeroufly ill. Her fon was alfo fick at the fame time; and died. He was a youth of

uncommon

uncommon accomplifhments, and fondly beloved by his parents. Arria prepared and conducted his funeral in such a manner, that her hufband remained entirely ignorant of the mournful event, which occafioned that folemnity. Pætus often inquired, with anxiety, about his fon; to whom fhe cheerfully replied, that he had flept well, and was better. But if her tears, too long reftrained, were burfting forth, fhe inftantly retired, to give vent to her grief; and when again compofed, fhe returned to Pætus with dry eyes, and a placid countenance, quitting, as it were, all the tender feelings of the mother, at the threfhold of her hufband's chamber. *

But, addreffing himfelf to Sophron, is it not a fpecies of equivocation, and .a breach of faithfulnefs, continued Phi-locles, when we do not perform our. promifes, according to the plain and obvious meaning of them ?

* Plin. Epift. XVI. Lib. III.

Without

Without doubt it is, anfwered Sophron. The moralift whom I before quoted, relates, that ten Romans, who had been taken in the battle of Cannæ, were fent by Hannibal to the fenate, to propofe an exchange of prifoners. Before they fet out, each of them engaged, by an oath, to return to the camp of the Carthaginians, if the embaffy fhould prove ineffectual. The fenate rejected the offers of Hannibal; and nine of the prifoners honourably rendered themfelves up to him. But the tenth refufed to return, on pretence, that he had already difcharged himfelf of his oath. For it feems, that he went back to the camp of the Carthaginians, foon after he quitted it, to fetch fome neceffaries, which he had defignedly left behind, that he might be able to plead his having complied, literally, with the terms of his engagement. But the fenate difdained the deceit, and commanded the artful wretch to be fent bound to Hannibal.

E　　　　　　　Mental,

Mental, and other private refervations neither abfolve, nor even extenuate the guilt of lying. When the unfortunate Mary queen of Scotland was married to the dauphin of France, the king, his father, folemnly ratified every article, infifted upon by the Scotch parliament, for preferving the independence of their nation, and for fecuring the fucceffion of the crown to the houfe of Hamilton. But Mary, by his perfuafion, had antecedently and privately fubfcribed three deeds, by which, fhe configned the kingdom of Scotland, on failure of her own iffue, to his family; declaring all her promifes, to the contrary, to be void.* The remark of Bifhop Taylor may be adopted, as the beft comment on tranfactions of this infamous nature. If the words be a *lie* without *refervation*, they are fo with it: For this does not alter the words themfelves; nor the meaning

* Lord Kaims's Hiftory of Man, Vol. IV. p. 158.

of

of the words; nor the purpofe of him who delivers them.*

But in what light are we to regard the ftratagems, falfhood, and acts of deceit, which have been employed in war, and often with applaufe, both in ancient and modern times?

In reply to this interefting queftion, Philocles obferved, that war is feldom founded in juftice; and that, therefore, we cannot be furprifed that it fhould occafion, amongft thofe who wage it, a fufpenfion of the common laws of morality. The fraudulent exploits which are practifed, by the tacit confent, as it were, of the parties, may dazzle and furprife a fuperficial obferver; but a ferious, honeft mind, will generally condemn them, as inconfiftent with the obligations of religion and virtue; and, except under very particular circum-

* Ductor Dubitant. p. 498.

 ftances,

ftances, injurious to the contending powers themfelves. For, as integrity is the beft policy in the conduct of individuals towards each other, it will appear to be equally fo in the tranf-actions between ftates, and communities, if an extenfive view be taken of their great and permanent interefts. Cicero, in one of his dialogues, introduces Scipio as maintaining the following excellent maxim: *non modo* FALSUM *effe illud,* SINE INJURIA *non poffe, fed hoc veriffimum, fine* SUMMA JUSTITIA *rempublicam regi non poffe.* " It is fo far from being true, that " government cannot be carried on with- " out injury to others, that nothing is " more certain, than that it cannot be " well adminiftered without an inviolable " adherence to the ftricteft juftice." And the propriety of this obfervation feems to be acknowledged, in fome of the regulations of war, now univerfally adopted in civilized countries.

But

But a diſtinction ſhould be made, between art or ſtratagem, and perfidy or
falſhood.* The wiſeſt and beſt moraliſts
admit, that we may deceive our enemies, when we have a juſt cauſe of war,
by any ſuch ſigns, as import no profeſſion
of communicating our ſentiments to
them. Thus I have heard, that the duke
of Marlborough, when he commanded
the allied army in Germany, called a
council of war, on a particular occaſion,
to determine whether he ſhould attack
the enemy on the ſucceeding day. His
general officers were unanimous in re-
commending the meaſure; but the duke
expreſſed his objections to it in the
ſtrongeſt terms; and the council ſub-
mitted to his ſuperior judgment. When
he retired into his tent, prince Eugene
followed him, and lamented the diſ-
grace, in which ſuch a deciſion would
involve them. " My reſolution," ſaid
the duke, " is fixed to give battle to-

* See Appendix, Sect. VII.

E 3

" morrow;

" morrow ; and I ſhall inſtantly iſſue
" the neceſſary orders. But I oppoſed
" this plan in council, becauſe I had re-
" ceived ſecret information, that our
" enemies had concerted the means of
" becoming acquainted with the reſult
" of our deliberations. And you will
" agree with me in the neceſſity of de-
" ceiving them."

But men of true courage and honour,
muſt hold in deteſtation all treachery and
falſhood. The earl of Peterborough, in
conjunction with the prince of Darmſtadt,
carried on the ſiege of Barcelona, about
the beginning of the preſent century.
The governor offered to capitulate, and
came to a parley with lord Peterborough
at the gates of the city. The articles
were not yet ſigned ; when ſuddenly
loud ſhouts and huzzas were heard in
the town. " You have perfidiouſly betrayed us !" ſaid the governor to the earl :
" Whilſt we are capitulating, with un-

" ſuſpecting

" ſuſpecting honour and ſincerity, your
" Engliſh ſoldiers have entered the city
" by the ramparts; and are now com-
" mitting rapine, murder, and every kind
" of violence." " You do injuſtice to
" the Engliſh," replied the general:
" This treachery is chargeable only on
" the troops of Darmſtadt. But permit
" me to enter into the town with my
" ſoldiers, and I will inſtantly repreſs
" the outrage, and return to the gate
" to finiſh the capitulation."

The offer was made with an air of truth, and ſincerity; and accepted with a generous confidence. Peterborough haſtened into the ſtreets, where he found the Germans and Catalans pillaging the houſes of the principal inhabitants. He drove them away; and obliged them to leave the booty, which they were carrying off: And, after having quieted all diſturbances, he rejoined the governor, and completed the capitulation, without de-

manding

manding any new, or more advantageous terms. The Spaniards were aftonifhed at the magnanimity of the Englifh, whom they had generally regarded before as faithlefs barbarians.*

Sophron remarked, that the glory, on this occafion, appeared to belong chiefly to lord Peterborough, as an individual. But I recollect, continued he, a tranfaction in the Grecian hiftory, which feems to evince an equal fenfe of honour, and deteftation of perfidy, in the whole body of the Athenians. Thefe people were inflamed with the ambition of governing Greece; and Themiftocles, a favourite general, exerted all his talents to accomplifh the defign. One day he affembled the citizens of Athens, and informed them, he had a moft important plan to propofe; but that he could not communicate it to them, becaufe the fuccefs of it depended upon

* See Voltaire's Siecle de Louis XIV.

fecrecy.

fecrecy. He therefore requefted them to appoint a confidential perfon, to whom he might explain his views, and whofe approbation of them might have the force of public authority. Ariftides was unanimoufly chofen; and Themiftocles laid open to him the projeƈt, which he had conceived, of burning the whole fleet of the Grecian ftates, then lying unguarded in a neighbouring port; the deftruƈtion of which, he faid, could not fail to fecure the dominion of Athens. Ariftides returned to the affembly, and declared, that the projeƈt of Themiftocles promifed the greateft benefit to the commonwealth; but that it was perfidious and unjuft. The people inftantly, and with one voice, rejeƈted the propofal. But the Athenians were foon afterwards corrupted by profperity: And Thucydides informs us, it became, with them, a maxim of ftate, " that " nothing is difhonourable, which is " advantageous." *

* Thucydid. Lib. VI.

Here

Here I could not forbear to mention
a noble, and long-continued exertion
of public faith and commercial honour,
though it was a flight digreffion from
the topic of difcourfe. The Spanifh
galeons, deftined to fupply Tierra Firma,
and the kingdoms of Peru and Chili,
with almoft every article of neceffary
confumption, touch firft at Carthagena,
and then at Porto-Bello. In the latter
place a fair is opened; the wealth of
America is exchanged for the manufac-
tures of Europe; and, during its prefcribed term of forty days, the richeft
traffic on the face of the earth is begun
and finifhed, with unbounded confidence,
and the utmoft fimplicity of tranfaction.
No bale of goods is ever opened, no cheft
of treafure is examined. Both are received on the credit of the perfons to
whom they belong; and only one inftance of fraud is recorded, during the
long period in which trade was carried on
with this liberal confidence. All the

coined

coined filver which was brought from Peru to Porto-Bello in the year 1654, was found to be adulterated, and to be mingled with a fifth part of bafe metal. The Spanifh merchants, with their ufual integrity, fuftained the whole lofs, and indemnified the foreigners by whom they were employed. The fraud was detected; and the treafurer of the revenue in Peru, the author of it, was publicly burnt.*

Are we not every day guilty of lying, purfued Philocles, in the common forms of civility; and in various modes of fpeech, which cuftom has introduced?

Surely not, replied Sophron; for if thefe be well underftood, no one is deceived by them.

I do not entirely accord with you, Sophron, faid I; and I believe it will not be eafy to juftify, upon the principles

* Robertfon's Hift. of America, Vol. II. Note 93. B. 8.

either

either of wifdom or ftrict morality, many complimental expreffions ufed in conver- fation. You remember the letter of the ambaffador from Bantam, which is in- ferted in one of the volumes of the Spec- tator. This honeft ftranger informs his mafter, that the people of England call him and his fubjects barbarians, becaufe they fpeak the truth; and account them- felves polite and civilized, becaufe they fay one thing, and mean another. "On " my firft landing," fays he, " one told " me that he fhould be glad to do me " any fervice in his power. I defired " him therefore to carry my portman- " teau; but inftead of ferving me ac- " cording to his promife, he laughed, " and ordered another to do it. I lodg- " ed the firft week at the houfe of a per- " fon, who intreated me to think myfelf " at home, and to confider his houfe as " my own. Accordingly, the next morn- " ing I began to knock down one of the " walls, in order to let in the frefh air;
" and

" and packed up some of the houshold
" goods, of which I intended to make
" thee a present. But the false varlet
" soon sent me word, that he would have
" no such doings in his house." Perhaps, however, I may incur the charge
of falshood, by quoting the letter of an
ambassador, who never existed.

Such fictions, Philocles remarked, partake not of the nature of lies. They
are intended to convey amusement or in-
struction, not to serve the purposes of
deceit.

Nor is the case essentially different,
with respect to the common forms of
civility. Their import is known to all
who use them; and, as they are expressive
of urbanity and benevolence, they tend,
under proper restrictions, to soften the
asperities, and heighten the pleasures
of social intercourse. Genuine courtesy
has, indeed, its seat in the heart; and
implies

implies the defire of gratifying others, in the fubordinate offices of life, by the facrifice of our own eafe or intereft. It is effential, therefore, to every amiable character; and can only difplay itfelf in fuch appropriated modes as cuftom has eftablifhed in different countries, or amongft different ranks of men. But, when the *fubftance* is wanting, fome benefit is derived to the world even from its *forms:* And to the ruftic, who claims the privilege of fpeaking improper truths, or of acting with rude and malicious fincerity, we may juftly addrefs the words of Shakefpear:

------------------ " This is fome fellow,
" Who, having been praifed for bluntnefs, doth affect
" A faucy roughnefs, and conftrains the garb
" Quite from his nature. He can't flatter, he,
" An honeft mind and plain; he muft fpeak truth,
" An they will take it fo; if not, 'tis plain."

On this account, I cannot but condemn the affected feverity of Paulinus, bifhop

of

of Nola, who reproves his correspondent Sulpicius Severus, for having subscribed himself his servant. " Beware," says this primitive writer, " thou subscribe " not thyself HIS SERVANT, who is thy " BROTHER; for flattery is sinful; and " it is not a testimony of humility, to " give those honours to men, which are " only due to the One Lord, Master, " and God."* We find the patriarch Abraham actuated by no such scruples, though he lived in the period of pastoral simplicity, and was highly distinguished for his virtue and integrity. " *And he* " *lift up his eyes, and looked; and lo, three* " *men stood by him: And when he saw them,* " *he ran to meet them from the tent door,* " *and bowed himself toward the ground;* " *and said, My lord, if now I have found* " *favour in thy sight, pass not away, I pray* " *thee, from thy servant.*"†

* See Barclay's Apology, p. 525.

† Genesis, Chap. xviii. Ver. 2, 3.

Lot,

Lot, alfo, is reprefented, in the book of Genefis, as accofting, in fimilar terms, two ftrangers, with whofe dignity he was then unacquainted. *" And he faid,* *" Behold now, my lords, turn in, I pray* *" you, into your fervant's houfe, and tarry* *" all night, and wafh your feet; and ye* *" fhall rife up early, and go on your ways."**

The conduct and expreffions of thefe venerable patriarchs, might, I obferved, be perfectly confiftent with the niceft adherence to truth and fincerity. For though they ftiled themfelves the *fervants* of the ftrangers, whom they addreffed, they could not mean to extend the term beyond fuch *fervices,* as the laws of hof-pitality required.

Similar laws, anfwered Philocles, which general confent has eftablifhed, bind every man, in the common inter-courfe of life, to reftrain his angry

* Genefis, Chap. xix. Ver. 2.

paffions,

paffions, to filence his fevere judgments, to fupprefs his pride and arrogance, and not only to correct whatever is offenfive in his manners, but to fhew that urbanity of fpirit, which, by its benevolent attentions, contributes to alleviate mifery, and to increafe the fum of public happinefs and order. Miftake me not, however, by fuppofing that I would recommend forward profeffions, a fawning demeanour, or unlimited complaifance. Integrity of heart, and fteadinefs of principle, forbid all finful conformity with the world: And I would neither flatter folly, countenance vice, nor yield up one important duty to artificial politenefs. But the facrifice of my own pride, refentment, caprice, or ill nature, to focial eafe and enjoyment, may often be required: And he, who, like Diogenes, neither poffeffes the fubftance, nor the form of courtefy, fhould be banifhed from the world. This Cynic, you remember, when he paid a vifit to Plato,

F

who

who united a tafte for elegance with the love of philofophy, exulted in the rudenefs of reproof, and bedaubing with his dirty feet the fine carpet, which covered the floor, cried out, " Thus I trample on the pride of Plato." " But with far greater pride," retorted Plato, with a farcaftic feverity, which the occafion fully justified. Lord Bacon mentions two noblemen of his acquaintance, one of whom kept a very magnificent table, but treated his guefts with illiberal freedom : The other, when he entertained the fame guefts, probably with humbler cheer, but more politenefs, ufed to afk them, " Tell truly, was there never a flout, or dry blow given at my lord's table ?" To which the guefts anfwered, " Such and fuch a thing paffed." " I thought," faid this nobleman, " he would mar a good dinner."*

Urbanity has been admirably characterifed, by a celebrated writer, under

* Bacon's Effays, XXXII.

the

the appellation of GENTLENESS. " This
virtue," he obferves, " is founded on a
" fenfe of what we owe to Him who
" made us, and to the common nature
" of which we all fhare. It arifes from
" reflection on our own failures and
" wants; and from juft views of the
" condition and the duty of man. It is
" native feeling, heightened, and im-
" proved by principle. It is the heart,
" which eafily relents; which feels for
" every thing that is human; and is
" backward and flow to inflict the leaft
" wound. It is affable in its addrefs,
" and mild in its demeanour; ever ready
" to oblige, and willing to be obliged
" by others; breathing habitual kindnefs
" towards friends, courtefy to ftrangers,
" long fuffering to enemies. It exer-
" cifes authority with moderation; ad-
" minifters reproof with tendernefs; con-
" fers favours with eafe and modefty. It
" is unaffuming in opinion, and tem-
" perate in zeal. It contends not eagerly

F 2

" about

" about trifles; flow to contradict, and
" still flower to blame; but prompt to
" allay diffention, and to restore peace.
" It neither intermeddles unneceffarily
" with the affairs, nor pries inquifitively
" into the fecrets, of others. It delights
" above all things to alleviate diftrefs,
" and, if it cannot dry up the falling
" tear, to footh at leaft the grieving
" heart. Where it has not the power of
" being ufeful, it is never burdenfome.
" It feeks to pleafe, rather than to fhine
" and dazzle; and conceals with care
" that fuperiority, either of talents or
" of rank, which is oppreffive to thofe
" who are beneath it. In a word, it is
" that fpirit, and that tenour of manners,
" which the Gofpel of Chrift enjoins,
" when it commands us *to bear one ano-*
" *ther's burdens; to rejoice with thofe who*
" *rejoice, and to weep with thofe who weep;*
" *to pleafe every one his neighbour for his*
" *good; to be kind and tender-hearted; to*

" *be*

*" be pitiful and courteous; to support the " weak, and to be patient towards all men."**

Sophron appeared to be much impreſſed with this animated and ſtriking picture of courteſy; but he ſuggeſted to Philocles, that amongſt the inferior offices of ſocial life, he had not noticed the duties of COUNSEL and REPROOF. Theſe, ſaid he, I fear, cannot be adminiſtered by a mind under the influence of gentleneſs, without the concealment, and ſometimes, even the violation of truth.

The former part of your allegation, replied Philocles, may perhaps be granted; but the latter I cannot admit. Advice and reprehenſion require, indeed, the utmoſt delicacy; and painful truths ſhould be delivered in the ſofteſt terms, and expreſſed no farther, than is neceſſary to produce their due effect. A courteous man will alſo mix what is conciliating,

* Blair's Sermons, Vol. I. p. 150.

F 3

with

with what is offensive ; praise, with cen-
sure ; deference and respect, with the
authority of admonition, so far as these
can be done in consistence with probity
and honour. For the mind revolts against
all censorian power, which displays pride
or pleasure in finding fault ; and is
wounded by the bare suspicion of such
disgraceful tyranny. But advice, divested
of the harshness, and yet retaining the
honest warmth, of truth, " is like honey,
put round the brim of a vessel full of
wormwood."* Even this vehicle, however, is sometimes insufficient to conceal
the draught of bitterness ; of which we
are furnished with an admirable and
diverting instance, in the history of Gil
Blas. This young man became the favourite of the archbishop of Grenada ;
in whose family he enjoyed a lucrative
and agreeable office; and future prospects
of much higher preferment. The archbishop regarded him as a person of taste

* Memoirs of Brandenburgh, by the King of Prussia.

and

and fentiment; and one day entered into
the following converfation with him.
" Liften, with attention, to what I am
" going to deliver.   My chief pleafure
" confifts in preaching; the Lord gives
" a blefling to my homilies; they touch
" the hearts of finners; make them fe-
" rioufly reflect on their conduct, and
" have recourfe to inftant repentance.
" This fuccefs fhould alone be a fuffi-
" cient incitement to my ftudies: never-
" thelefs, I will confefs to thee my weak-
" nefs, and acknowledge, that I propofe
" to myfelf another reward; a reward,
" with which the delicacy of my nature
" reproaches me in vain.   The honour
" of being reckoned a perfect orator, has
" charmed my imagination: My per-
" formances are thought equally nervous
" and refined; but I am anxious to avoid
" the misfortune of thofe who write too
" long; and I wifh to retire without
" forfeiting one tittle of my reputation.
" Wherefore, my dear Gil Blas, what

I exact

" I exact of thy zeal, is, that whenever
" thou shalt perceive a failure in my
" genius, or the least mark of the imbe-
" cility of old age in my compositions,
" that thou wilt immediately advertise
" me of it. I dare not trust to my own
" judgment, which may be seduced by
" self-love; but make choice of thine,
" because I know it to be good, and
" am resolved to stand by thy decision."

Some time after this discourse, the
prelate was seized with a fit of apoplexy.
He was, however, soon relieved; and
such salutary medicines were administered,
that his health seemed to be re-established.
But his understanding suffered a severe
shock, which was plainly perceptible in
the first homily that he composed. The
succeeding one proved perfectly decisive;
as it abounded in repetitions, vain arguments, and false pathos. " Now," said
Gil Blas to himself, " master homily-
" critic, prepare to exercise the office,
" which

" which you have undertaken. You fee
" that the faculties of his grace begin
" to fail. It is your duty to give him
" notice of it, not only as the depofitory
" of his thoughts, but likewife, left you
" fhould be anticipated by fome other
" of his friends." But the embarraff-
ment was, how to convey the mortifying
intimation to his patron. Fortunately,
the archbifhop extricated him from the
difficulty, by inquiring, what people faid
of him, and if they were fatisfied with
his laft difcourfe. Gil Blas anfwered,
that the homily had not fucceeded fo well
as the others, in affecting the audience.
" How," replied the prelate, with aftonifhment, " has it met with any Ariftarchus?"
" No, fir," faid Gil Blas, " by no means:
" But fince you have laid your injunctions
" upon me to be open and fincere, I
" will take the liberty of telling you,
" that your late difcourfe, in my judg-
" ment, has not altogether the energy of
" your prior performances." The archbifhop

bishop grew pale at these words; and said, with a forced smile, "So then, "Mr. Gil Blas, this piece is not to your "taste? You think my understanding "enfeebled, don't you?" "I should not have spoken so freely," answered Gil Blas, "if your grace had not com-"manded me. I do no more, therefore, "than obey you; and I most humbly "beg that you will not be offended at "my freedom." "God forbid," cried the prelate, with precipitation; "God "forbid, that I should find fault with it. "This would be extremely unjust. I am "not angry, that you speak your senti-"ments: it is the sentiment only that "I condemn. Know, that I never com-"posed a better homily, than that, which "you disapprove; for my genius, thank "Heaven, hath yet lost nothing of its "vigour. Henceforth, however, I will "chuse an abler confidant than you are. "Go," added he, pushing Gil Blas out of his closet, by the shoulders; "go, "tell my treasurer to give you a hundred

"ducats.

" ducats. I wifh you all manner of
" profperity, with a little more tafte."*

But we have enlarged fufficiently on
this part of our fubject. Permit me,
therefore, Sophron, to proceed, by inquiring, whether SECRECY, in certain
cafes, be not a branch of faithfulnefs,
or veracity?

It is a very important one, anfwered
Sophron. To betray the confidence that
is repofed in us, whether we have tacitly,
or by a promife, bound ourfelves to
fidelity, evinces a weak underftanding,
or a bad heart. Levity, an eagernefs
to communicate, or the defire of feeming to be important, are the moft frequent caufes of the breach of fecrecy;
but it is to be feared, that it fometimes
originates from bafenefs and malevolence.

This offence was deemed infamous
by the ancient Perfians. For it was

* Gil Blas, Vol. III.

their

their opinion, fays Quintus Curtius, that however deficient a man might be in the talents, requifite to the attainment of excellency, the negative virtues were, at leaft, in his power; and that he might be filent, although he could not be eloquent.

Here Philocles judicioufly remarked, that the laws of fecrecy are not, in all cafes, to be regarded as inviolable; for we are under antecedent obligations, of a nature ftill more forcible and binding. If any atrocious defign, either againft an individual or the ftate, be communicated in confidence to us, it is our duty to diffuade the party, if poffible, from the execution of it. But fhould our endeavours appear to be unavailing, the concealment of what we know, might involve us in the guilt of the offence; and we fhould be juftly punifhable, as acceffaries to the crime.* At Florence,

* See Appendix, Sect. IX.

and

and in other ſtates of Italy, a man apprifed of a plot againſt the government, is put to death for not revealing it.* In England, *miſpriſion* of *treaſon* is puniſhed, by forfeiture of rents, and of goods, and by impriſonment during life: And *miſpriſion* of *felony*, by impriſonment for a diſcretionary term, and by fine and ranſom, at the pleaſure of the king's judges.†

If ſuch *miſpriſions* be really culpable, how comes it to paſs, I aſked, that informers are almoſt univerſally held in contempt and deteſtation?

Becauſe few villains, ſaid Philocles, will communicate their wicked defigns to any but thoſe, whom they believe inclined to participate in the commiſſion of them.   Hence there is generally a preſumption of previous guilt in the

* Guiccardini's Hiſt.

† Blackſtone's Commentaries.

informer:

informer: And to this guilt, we super-
add that of bafenefs and perfidy; as we
are not willing to fuppofe that he is
influenced to perform this public act,
either by motives of private virtue, or
of patriotifm. However, we fhould be
careful not to carry our prepoffeffion
againft informers, even of this clafs,
too far. They do effential fervice to the
community; and may, perhaps, think
this fervice the beft atonement for their
paft guilt, and the fulleft proof of their
prefent repentance.

There is another branch of faithfulnefs,
which it is alfo difhonourable to violate; and which lays us under an obligation to avoid TATTLING, TALE-BEARING,
and CENSORIOUSNESS. In the unguarded
hours of focial intercourfe, and ftill more
in the commerce of domeftic life, the
wifeft and the beft of men fpeak their
thoughts without referve; and cafting
off all reftraint, may fometimes deviate,

both

both in their words and actions, from the rules of ſtrict propriety. To relate ſuch inadvertencies, is meanneſs ; to ridicule them, is ill nature ; and to exaggerate them, is calumny.*

Sophron now turned our attention to a moſt important branch of moral Truth, by inquiring whether INSINCERITY in RELIGION may not be deemed a highly criminal ſpecies of lying ?

Certainly it may, returned Philocles. GOD is a being of ſpotleſs purity, who ſearches the heart, and commands us to worſhip him *" in ſpirit and in truth."* *" Lying lips,"* whether employed in falſe profeſſions of faith or of piety, *" are an abomination to the Lord."* And he who

* *Abſentem qui rodit Amicum,*
  Qui non defendit, alio culpante, ſolutos
  Qui captat riſus hominum, famamque dicacis,
  Fingere qui non viſa poteſt, commiſſa tacere
  Qui nequit; hic Niger eſt; hunc tu, Romane, caveto.
  Hor. Lib. 1. Sat. 4.

can,

can, habitually, practise insincerity and hypocrify, in thofe ferious and important tranfactions with his Creator, Benefactor, and Judge, which have eternity for their object, is not likely to pay any fteady regard to temporary interefts, refulting from the laws of fociety, or the ordinary obligations of morality. When one of the kings of France folicited M. Bougier, who was a proteftant, to conform to the Roman Catholic religion, promifing him, in return, a commiffion or a government, " Sire," replied he, " if I could be perfuaded to betray my " God for a marfhal's ftaff, I might be " induced to betray my king for a bribe " of much lefs value."

It was a noble reply! cried Sophron, with ingenuous warmth; and the recital of it brings to my memory a ftory, which the duke of Sully has recorded of Ambrofe Parè, a zealous Huguenot, and furgeon to Charles the Ninth of France.

He

He was with the king, during the time of the maſſacre of Paris, when ſo many thouſand innocent and virtuous perſons were inhumanly butchered in cold blood; and was perhaps a witneſs of the monarch's firing with a carabine, upon the wretched Calviniſts, who fled from their murderers by the windows of the palace. The courtiers, as they came into the royal preſence, vied with each other, in boaſting of the barbarities which they had committed; and Charles ſaid to Parè, whoſe religious opinions he well knew, " The time is now come, when " I ſhall have none but catholics in my " dominions." " Sire," anſwered he, without embarraſſment or perturbation, " can you forget your promiſe to me, " that I ſhould never be obliged to go " to maſs!" The duke of Sully ſeems to be of opinion, that the edict, which Charles iſſued the ſucceeding day, to prohibit the continuance of the maſſacre, was partly owing to the intrepidity and influence of Parè.

G

The

The conduct of Parè, said Philocles, on so trying an occasion, affords a striking proof of firmness and sincerity, in the profession of religious faith. But examples, of much higher degrees of similar fidelity, are to be found in the earlier annals of the Christian church. Nor are instances wanting, even in the heathen world, of a zealous and fearless attachment to those rites, which ignorance deemed sacred, and which individuals or bodies of men bound themselves, by solemn engagements, to perform. When the Gauls were become masters of Rome, they besieged the capitol, and closely guarded every avenue, to prevent the escape of a single Roman citizen. Under these circumstances of danger, Caius Fabius Dorso, a young man of an illustrious family, descended from the capitol, bearing certain holy utensils in his hands; and passed through the midst of the enemy, regardless of their menaces, to offer a sacrifice to the gods

gods on the hill Quirinalis. This facrifice, it was the cuſtom of his anceſtors to perform yearly, on a ſtated day; and when he had finiſhed the ſolemnity, the Gauls, though a fierce and barbarous people, ſuffered him to return unmoleſted, admiring his piety, and aſtoniſhed at his intrepidity.* Facts, like theſe, ſhould make us bluſh at indifference, and abhor diſſimulation in religion. But whilſt we allow ſuch impreſſions to produce their full influence on our hearts, let us beware of paſſing judgment upon others, with raſhneſs or unchriſtian ſeverity. Intemperate zeal is apt to beget a malignancy of ſpirit, no leſs incompatible with the love of GOD, than with benevolence to man. The conviction of the mind, in matters of faith, often depends more upon education and authority, than on the exertions of reaſon: And if we ſee men profeſſing to believe,

* Vid. Liv. Hiſt.

what

what is unintelligible or abfurd, we
fhould be well affured that they have
not deceived themfelves, before we ac-
cufe them of mocking their Creator, and
impofing on the world.

We may pity ignorance, and lament
credulity; but hypocrify, urged Sophron,
merits from us no indulgence: And this
fpecies of falfhood is fo characteriftically
marked, that it cannot be miftaken.
Who, that obferves a man fanctified in
his behaviour, and affiduous in his public
devotions, whilft he is at the fame time
felfifh, malevolent, bigoted, and oppreffive, will hefitate to charge him with
the groffeft and moft infamous diffimulation?

If there be fufficient proof, that this
is really his temper of mind, I acknowledge, faid Philocles, that you may and
ought to brand him with the name of
hypocrite. But no man fhould be charged
with

with a crime univerſally odious, on ſlight or equivocal evidence.* There is a ſpecies of devotion, which, having its ſeat chiefly in the imagination and the paſſions, bears no exact proportion to the virtue of the character in which it is found: And charity, together with a humble ſenſe of our own infirmities, will always lead us to put the moſt favourable conſtruction on the conduct of our fellow creatures. We ſhould remember alſo, that enthuſiaſm and ſuperſtition have often appeared, with the external marks of diſſimulation. The famous lord Herbert, of Cherbury, had written an elaborate work againſt Chriſtianity, which he intitled, *De Veritate, prout diſtinguitur à Revelatione.* But knowing that it would meet with much oppoſition, he remained ſome time in anxious ſuſpence about the publication of it. Providence, however, as he informs us, kindly interpoſed,

---

* See Appendix, Sect. X.

 and

and determined his wavering refolu-
tions. Hear the marvellous tale, which
he relates !

"Being thus doubtful in my chamber,
"one fair day in the fummer, my cafe-
"ment being opened towards the fouth,
"the fun fhining clear, and no wind
"ftirring, I took my book *De Veritate*
"in my hand, and kneeling on my
"knees, devoutly faid, *O thou eternal*
"*God, I am not fatisfied enough whether I*
"*fhall publifh this book; if it be for thy*
"*glory, I befeech thee give me fome fign from*
"*heaven; if not, I fhall fupprefs it.* I had
"no fooner fpoken thefe words, but a
"loud, though yet gentle noife, came
"from the heavens, which did fo com-
"fort and cheer me, that I took my
"petition as granted, and that I had the
"fign I demanded; whereupon alfo I
"refolved to print my book." *

* See the Life of Lord Herbert, written by himfelf.

It

It muſt appear ſtrange, that a man, who had ſpent a conſiderable part of his life in courts and camps, ſhould poſſeſs ſuch a deluded imagination. And this deluſion will be ſtill more ſuſpicious, when you are told, that lord Herbert's chief argument againſt Chriſtianity is, the improbability that Heaven ſhould reveal its laws only to a portion of the earth. For how could he, who doubted of a *partial*, believe an *individual* revelation? Or is it poſſible, that he could have the vanity to think his book of ſuch importance, as to extort a declaration of the Divine will, when the intereſt and happineſs of a fourth part of mankind, were deemed, by him, objects inadequate to the like diſplay of goodneſs?* Do theſe arguments convince you of lord Herbert's hypocriſy? Your concluſion is haſty, and unjuſt. Read his life, and you will be ſatisfied, that

* See Walpole's Cat. of Royal and Noble Authors.

the

the warmth of his temper might expofe him to felf-deception; but that he was incapable of obtruding on the world, what he knew to be a falfhood.

Sophron modeftly acknowledged, that the figns of religious diffimulation might be lefs decifive, than he had fuppofed. But allow me, faid he, to contraft your inftance of lord Herbert, with two facts concerning Oliver Cromwell; to fhew that the charge of hypocrify may be juftly grounded on fingle actions, without taking into our view the whole tenour of a man's life. Suppofe a ftranger, ignorant of the craftinefs and ambition of Cromwell, to have been prefent in the long parliament, when the ordinance for the trial of Charles I. was read and affented to; would he have hefitated to think him an hypocrite, after hearing him deliver the following words? " Should any one have volun- " tarily propofed to bring the king to

" punifh-

" punifhment, I fhould have regarded
" him as the greateft traitor; but fince
" Providence and neceffity have caft us
" upon it, I will pray to God for a blef-.
" fing on your councils; though I am
" not prepared to give you my advice
" on this important occafion. Even I
" myfelf, when I was lately offering up
" a petition for his majefty's reftoration,
" felt my tongue cleave to the roof of
" my mouth; and confidered this fuper-
" natural movement, as the anfwer which
" Heaven, having rejected the king,
" had fent to my fupplications." *

Let us further fuppofe, that this
ftranger attended the high court of juftice, and faw Cromwell, when he took
the pen in his hand, to fign the warrant
for the king's execution, jocularly be-
daub the face of his neighbour with the
ink; could he forbear to exprefs his
difguft at the levity which he then ob-

* Whitlock.

ferved;

ferved; and his abhorrence of the grofs diffimulation, to which he had been before a witnefs?

You have drawn your example, replied Philocles, from that diftracted period of our hiftory, when truth appears to have been banifhed from public life. The defpotic views of a monarch, who was under the influence of a popifh queen, a bigoted prelate, and a corrupt ftatefman, led him to the practice of deceit and falfhood;* and the parties,

---

* Confult Clarendon, Vol. I. p. 22. Rufhworth, Vol. 1. from p. 119 to 127. Hume's Hift. 4to. Vol. I. p. 103. Ed. 1754. " He had promifed to the laft houfe of commons a redrefs of " this religious grievance; but he was too apt, in imitation " of his father, to confider thefe promifes as temporary ex- " pedients, which after the diffolution of the parliament, he " was not any farther to regard." Id. p. 156. See alfo the Life of the Lord Keeper Williams, p. 143. Whitlock, p. 10. The Petition of Rights. Harris's Hift. Sidney's State Papers, Vol. II. p 665, &c. Rapin fays, " Charles made frequent " ufe of mental refervations, concealed in ambiguous terms, " and general expreffions, of which he referved the explica- " tion to a proper time and place. For this reafon, the par- " liament could never confide in his promifes, wherein there " was

who united in opposing his encroach-
ments on the civil and religious rights
of the people, soon deviated from their
original principles; and availing themselves of the gloomy enthusiasm of the
times, concealed their perfidy and ambition, under the mask of pious zeal, and
divine

" was always either some ambiguous term, or some restriction
" that rendered them useless. This may be said to be one of
" the principal causes of his ruin; because giving thereby
" occasion of distrust, it was not possible to find any expedi-
" ent for a peace with the parliament. He was thought to
" act with so little sincerity in his engagements, that it was
" believed there was no dependence on his word. The
" parliament could not even resolve to debate on the king's
" propositions, so convinced were they of his ability to hide
" his real intentions, under ambiguous expressions." Rapin's
Hist. Vol. II. p. 570. The following passage is taken from
the works of an historian, who is acknowledged to have
been very partial to king Charles. " *Malè posita est lex, quæ*
" *tumultuariè posita est*, was one of those positions of Aristotle,"
says he, " which hath never since been contradicted; and
" was an advantage, that, being well managed, and stoutly
" insisted upon, would, in spite of all their machinations,
" which were not yet firmly and solidly formed, have brought
" them to a temper of being treated with. But I have some
" cause to believe, that even this argument, which was un-
" answerable for the rejecting that bill, was applied for the
" confirming it; and an opinion that the violence and force,
" used

divine illuminations. That Cromwell
was guilty of hypocrify, may with too
much probability be inferred from numerous and undoubted facts. But I
know not whether the two, which you
have related, would have authorifed a
ftranger to charge him publicly, with
this reproachful offence. Cromwell pof-

" ufed in procuring it, rendered it abfolutely invalid and void,
" made the confirmation of it lefs confidered, as not being of
" ftrength to make that act good, which was in itfelf null.
" And I doubt this logic had an influence upon other acts of
" lefs moment." Clarendon's Hift. Vol. II. p. 30. Rapin
makes the following obfervation on this paffage. " Let the
" reader judge after this, if we may boaft of king Charles's
" fincerity, fince even in paffing acts of parliament, which
" are the moft authentic and folemn promifes a king of
" England can make, he gave his affent, merely in an
" opinion, that they were void in themfelves, and confe-
" quently he was not bound by this engagement." I have
inferted thefe references and quotations, not merely to au-
thenticate my charge againft king Charles, but to fhew, from
his unhappy fate, how delufive, dangerous, and infamous,
is the following political obfervation of Machiavel. " It has
" appeared by experience, that thofe princes who have made
" light of their word, and artfully deceived mankind, have
" all along done great things, and have at length got the better
" of fuch as proceeded upon honourable principles."

feffed

feffed a vigorous, active, and enlarged underftanding; and could affume, whenever he pleafed, that dignity of manners, which befitted his high ftation. But when he relaxed himfelf from the toils of war, or the cares of government, his amufements frequently confifted in the loweft buffoonery. Yet in thefe apparently unguarded moments, he was upon the watch to remark the characters, defigns, and weakneffes of men; and to penetrate into the inmoft receffes of their hearts. Before the trial of Charles, a meeting was held between the chiefs of the republican party and the general officers, to concert the model of the intended new government. After the debates on this moft interefting and important fubject, Ludlow informs us, that Cromwell, by way of frolic, threw a cufhion at his head; and when Ludlow took up another cufhion to return the joke, the general ran down ftairs, and

was

was in danger of breaking his bones in the hurry.* It is evident, therefore, that this extraordinary man might really be ſerious, under the appearance of levity. But this topic has engroſſed too much of our attention: And I will only add, that the more we cultivate moral or religious ſincerity in ourſelves, the leſs diſpoſed we ſhall be to ſuſpect the want of it in others.

There is a character, ſaid Sophron, of genuine dignity and importance, not uſurped like that of Cromwell, the luſtre of which has been tarniſhed by the charge of religious diſſimulation. This charge, you know, is laid in the ſtrongeſt terms againſt the apoſtle Peter, by St. Paul himſelf, who writes thus to the Galatians: *" But when Peter came to Antioch, I with-* *" ſtood him to the face, becauſe he was to be* *" blamed. For before that certain came from*

" *James*

" *James, he did eat with the Gentiles; but*
" *when they were come, he withdrew, and*
" *separated himself, fearing them which were*
" *of the circumcision. And the other Jews*
" *dissembled likewise with him; insomuch*
" *that Barnabas was carried away with*
" *their dissimulation. But when I saw that*
" *they walked not uprightly, according to the*
" *Gospel, I said unto Peter before them all,*
" *If thou, being a Jew, livest after the*
" *manner of Gentiles, and not as do the Jews,*
" *why compellest thou the Gentiles to live*
" *as do the Jews?*"

.The conduct of Peter, on this occasion, is the more extraordinary, as he
appears to have had the fullest conviction
of the abolition of the Jewish ceremonies,
by the promulgation of the Gospel of
Christ:* A conviction, founded on an
immediate revelation from heaven; in
consequence of which he baptized the
centurion Cornelius and his family.

* Acts, Chap. v. Ver. 7, 8.

" *And*

" And he said unto them, Ye know how
" that it is an unlawful thing for a man
" that is a Jew, to keep company with, or
" come unto one of another nation; but God
" hath shewed me, that I should not call any
" man common or unclean: For of a truth
" I perceive that God is no respecter of
" persons: But in every nation, he that
" feareth him, and worketh righteousness, is
*" accepted with him."**

The enemies of Christianity, answered Philocles, have indecently and unjustly triumphed in this dispute between the apostles: And its friends, with a zeal no less heated and erroneous, have anxiously sought to disavow, or to evade it. Two primitive fathers† of the church, have even represented it as a stratagem or deceit, concerted privately, for the benefit of the Jewish converts: But Austin rejects this defence with proper

---

* Acts, Chap. x.

† Chrysostom and Jerom.

indigna-

indignation, as dishonourable to the character of Paul, and inadequate to the justification of Peter, whose conduct he confesses to have been worthy of reprehension. The truth, indeed, seems to be, that this great apostle suffered himself to be governed, on the unfortunate occasion now alluded to, as on several others of his life, by the warmth and impetuosity of his passions. But dissimulation is not the concomitant of such a temper of mind: And as the history of Peter sufficiently evinces, that this vice was foreign to his nature, it could originate only, in the present instance, from the sudden impression of fear on one, not yet completely disciplined in the school of fortitude. Let us learn, therefore, Sophron, from the severity of St. Paul's rebuke, to avoid all mean prevarications, or time-serving compliances, inconsistent with our religious principles; and "*to walk uprightly, according to the* " *truth of the Gospel; holding fast the liberty,* " *with which Christ has made us free.*"

H May

May we remember alfo, in the judgments which we form, concerning the faith and practices of others, that our great Mafter and Lawgiver has invefted them with the fame freedom, which we ourfelves enjoy; and that if an apoftle was not authorifed to impofe a yoke on others, we can have no claim to prefide over confcience, however erroneous it may be, or to affume any power in fpiritual matters, but what arifes from the perfuafive influence of fuperior reafon: And even in the exercife of this faculty, our language and treatment fhould be fuch, as to manifeft the benignity and gentlenefs of Chriftian toleration.

I could not hear the term *toleration* from the mouth of Philocles, without expreffing fome objections to it, although it has been adopted by Mr. Locke, and other writers of the firft diftinction. For words, I obferved, have a confiderable

influence

influence on opinions; and the present term appears to be injurious to that religious liberty, which it is designed to import. It implies a *right* to impose articles of faith, and modes of worship; that non-conformity is a crime; and that the *sufferance* of it is a matter of favour or lenity. But the non-conformist in every country, whether he be a Christian at Constantinople, a Protestant at Rome, an Episcopalian in Scotland, or a Presbyterian in England, if his rational principles be consonant to his practice, will regard this claim of *right* as usurpation, and will urge, that it has neither been conferred by Jesus Christ, nor delegated by the people. Our Saviour expressly declares, " *My kingdom is not of this world:* " And his religion was persecuted and oppressed, during the period of its greatest purity and perfection, and when the ministers of it had gifts and powers which are now unknown. The people could not delegate such a right

H 2

to

to any man, or body of men : For the human mind is fo mutable, that no individual can fix a ftandard of his own faith, much lefs can he commiffion another to eftablifh one for him and his pofterity. And this power would in no hands be fo dangerous, as in thofe of the ftatefman or prieft, who has the folly and prefumption to think himfelf qualified to exercife it.

Philocles, by his filence, feemed to acquiefce in what I had advanced : And when I apologifed, afterwards, for the interruption, which I had more than once occafioned, to the methodical difcuffion of the fubject in debate, he very politely replied, that the freedom of converfation admits not of a rigid adherence to the precife rules of fyftem. But were it otherwife, faid he, the mind is relieved from wearinefs, and animated to more attention, by feafonable digreffions, if not too long, or too often repeated.

That

That I am not averse to enter into them myself, you may already have observed, and will now find, by my recalling to Sophron's memory the dispute between the apostles Paul and Peter; and deducing from it an argument in favour of the truth of Christianity. It is obvious, I think, from this incident, that there was no combination to deceive mankind amongst the first preachers of the Gospel; and that if, on ordinary occasions, they were actuated by the common weaknesses and prejudices of human nature, they neither attempted to conceal, nor to extenuate them. With the simplicity of truth, they related facts, as they occurred, whether advantageous or otherwise to their characters. And every unprejudiced judge will discover, in the records of the Gospel, such internal marks of fidelity, as no other history, either of ancient or modern periods, can display. Justly, therefore, may we apply to the writings of the Evangelists, that maxim

H 3

of

of Cicero, " *Quis nescit primam esse historiæ*
" *legem, ne quid falsi dicere audeat ; deinde,*
" *ne quid veri, non audeat ?* " *

—— A pause ensued ; and the conversation seemed to be concluded. But
Sophron taking up Locke's Essay on
the Human Understanding, which happened to lie on the table before him, read
the distinction which that author makes,
between moral and metaphysical truth.
This suggested fresh matter of discussion,
and gave rise to a variety of observations,
on the danger of error, and on the conduct of reason in our intellectual pursuits. Philocles particularly enlarged
on the pernicious consequences of sup-
porting FALSE OPINIONS, for the sake of
argument, in public or private disputations ; and represented this practice as
one great source of scepticism and infide-
lity, amongst literary men.†   The ima-

* Cicero de Oratore, Lib. II.
† See Appendix, Sect. VI.

gination,

gination, said he, is struck with novelty; it appears honourable to shake off the fetters of vulgar prejudice; and pride is doubly gratified, by the humiliation of an opponent, and the triumph over authority. Thus the passions become engaged, on the side which the sceptic espouses; sophistry is mistaken for sound logic; he becomes enamoured of discoveries, made by his superior penetration; and the singularity of his notions, or principles, which would create doubt and hesitation in a wise man, tends only to strengthen his conviction of their certainty. Milton, describing the character of Belial, one of the fallen angels, says in emphatic language,

- - - - - - - - - - - - - - " His tongue
" Dropt manna, and could make the worse appear
" The better reason, to perplex and dash
" Maturest counsels." *

* Paradise Lost, Book II. L. 112.

Does

Does not the philofopher's maxim, faid Sophron, " *Nullius jurare in verba magiſtri,*" feem to recommend a ſtrict ſcrutiny into every ſubject? And what more judicious method can be deviſed, of correcting our prejudices, in favour of any eſtabliſhed opinion, than by ſetting ourſelves, boldly, in oppoſition to it?

Would you free yourſelf, Sophron, from a trifling malady, by incurring a fevere and dangerous one; then, urged Philocles, you may correct a ſlight prejudice by adopting another that is greater! In our inquiries into truth, we ought to diveſt ourſelves, as much as poſſible, of every prepoſſeſſion. But it is ſurely a reaſonable deference, to the judgment of the public, concerning any doctrine or opinion, that we ſhould firſt examine, with attention, the arguments in its favour, before we admit the objections which may be raiſed againſt it. And by this method the mind will

be

be leaſt unfairly biaſſed in her deciſions;
and will reſt on them, with a degree of
confidence and ſatisfaction, which can
never reſult from partial or prejudiced
inveſtigation. Young men of lively
parts and acute underſtandings, when
they enter upon the field of controverſy,
are ſometimes ſo proud of their polemic
ſkill, as to engage, indiſcriminately, on
any ſide of the queſtion in debate. This
is a dangerous practice, and cenſured
even by Socrates himſelf; whoſe labours
were devoted to the diſcuſſion of truth,
and the detection of error. "If thou
"continueſt to take delight in idle argu-
"mentation," ſaid he to Euclides, "thou
"mayeſt be qualified to combat with
"the ſophiſts, but wilt never know how
"to live with men." And lord Bacon,
the great luminary of ſcience, appears
to have entertained ſimilar ideas: For,
ſpeaking of the logic of Ariſtotle, he
terms it, "a philoſophy for contention
"only; but barren in the production
"of

"of works, for the benefit of life."*
Many lamentable proofs have I feen,
of the tendency of this habit of alterca-
tion to create indifference, not only to
intellectual, but alfo to moral and religious truth. Cato, the cenfor, pro-
phefied the ruin of the Roman conftitution, whenever this fort of learning
fhould become the fafhionable ftudy of
his countrymen. He conceived his dif-
like to it on the following occafion.
" In the year of Rome 599, the Athe-
" nians fent three of their principal phi-
" lofophers, on an embaffy to the re-
" public. At the head of thefe was
" Carneades, a very celebrated leader
" of the academic fect. While he was
" waiting for an anfwer from the fenate,
" he employed himfelf in difplaying his
" talents in the art of difputation: And
" the Roman youth flocked round him,
" in great numbers. In one of thefe
" public difcourfes he attempted to

* Biog. Brit. Vol. I. 2d Edit. p. 449.

" prove,

" prove, that *justice, and injustice, depend
" altogether on the institutions of civil society,
" and have no foundation in nature.* The
" next day, agreeably to the manner of
" that sect, and in order to set the argu-
" ments on each side of the question in
" full view, he supported with equal
" eloquence, the reverse of his former
" proposition. Cato was present at both
" these disputations; and being appre-
" hensive that the moral principles of
" the Roman youth might be shaken,
" if they should become converts to this
" mode of philosophising, he was anxious
" to prevent its reception; and did not
" rest, till he had prevailed with the
" senate to dismiss the ambassadors, with
" their final answer." *

Perhaps the versatile opinions and
principles of the Jesuits may be ascribed
to this cause; for I have been informed
by several of them, with whom I have

* *Plut. in Vit. Caton.* Melmoth's Cato, p, 190.

con-

converſed, that their academical exerciſes are chiefly directed to make them ſubtle diſputants. How far the ſame obſervation may be applicable to the members of a learned profeſſion, highly reſpected in this country, I will not preſume to determine. But there is too much reaſon to apprehend, that the cuſtom of pleading for any client, without diſcrimination of right or wrong, muſt leſſen the regard due to thoſe important diſtinctions, and deaden the moral ſenſibility of the heart. *

I have been too ſtrongly impreſſed with the love of truth, replied Sophron, to debate with indifference about it; and therefore to guard againſt deception, from " what the nurſe, and what the prieſt have taught," I would examine my moſt ſerious opinions, and try whether I cannot, by direct oppoſition, or

* See Appendix, Sect. VII.

by

by the teſt of ridicule, invalidate their
authority.

I have already given you my reaſons
againſt this practice; anſwered Philocles,
and I could enforce them by many examples of the pernicious conſequences
of it, which have fallen under my obſervation. But private hiſtory is invidi-
ous; and I ſhall therefore confine myſelf
to a few caſes of public notoriety. The
academy of Dijon, many years ago, pro-
poſed the following whimſical prize queſtion, viz. " Whether the ſciences may
" not be deemed more hurtful, than
" beneficial to ſociety?" M. Rouſſeau
became a candidate for the laurel, and
aſſumed the affirmative ſide of the queſtion; probably becauſe it furniſhed him
with a better opportunity of diſplaying
his genius, and powers of perſuaſion.*

* *Major eſt ille qui judicium abſtulit, quam qui meruit.* Cic.

Neſcio quomodo, dum lego aſſentior, cum poſui librum, aſſenſio emnis illa elabitur. Idem.

His

His difcourfe was received with the higheft applaufe; he became the dupe of his own rhetoric; and adopted as a philofopher, the maxims which he had delivered as an orator. From this period commenced his fame, his paradoxes, and his misfortunes.* He combated the common fenfe of mankind, with all the zeal of a reformer; and his writings proved like the bubble which glitters, expands, and burfts in the funfhine: They were dazzling, empty, and foon forgotten. I am inclined to fufpect that Machiavel's Prince, the Fable of the Bees, and other productions of this nature, originated from caufes fomewhat fimilar to thofe which gave rife to the chimæras of Rouffeau. And it is faid that a celebrated adverfary of Chriftianity, by yielding up his judgment and imagination to a particular fet of

* Helvetius.

arguments,

arguments, became fucceffively a proteftant, a papift, and an infidel.*

But permit me, Sophron, to fuggeft
to you a caution of ftill higher importance, which regards fuch of your intellectual purfuits as relate to the Deity.
Religion may be confidered both as a
fpeculative fcience, and as a practical
principle. In the former view, it conftitutes the fublimeft object of the underftanding, and the moft interefting
topic of rational inveftigation. In the
latter, it is a fpring of motion, and ex-
cites all the devout affections of veneration, gratitude, and love. When you
contemplate, as a philofopher, the character of the Divine Being, you muft
be ftruck with reverence at the proofs,
which offer themfelves, of his boundlefs
power, univerfal prefence, and infinite
duration: And thefe attributes, reflect-

* See an account of Mr. Tindal, in the Britifh Biography,
Vol. IX. p. 314.

ing

ing dignity and luftre on the more
amiable perfections of his nature, will
heighten the impreffion made by the
relation, which he ftands in to you, as
your Creator, Benefactor, and Friend.
Thus the principle of piety will fubfift
in your mind, in its full force; fupported
by the authority of reafon, and harmo-
nifing with all the feelings of your heart.
But if you defcend, from thefe general
and exalted views of the Divine Being,
into minute difquifitions concerning his
effence, the freedom of his agency, and
other fubtleties beyond the human ken,
you will foon damp the ardour of devotion in your breaft: And fhould you
make thefe inquiries the common matter
of academical difputation, or of familiar
debate, the facred flame will be extin-
guifhed altogether.* The poet, lately
quoted, has defcribed fome of the fallen
angels, who had been driven from

* See Dr. Gregory's Comparative View; and Mrs. Barbauld
on Devotional Tafte.

heaven

heaven for impiety and rebellion, as "fitting on a hill retired, and reasoning high"

" Of providence, foreknowledge, will, and fate,
" Fix'd fate, free will, foreknowledge absolute;
" And found no end, in wand'ring mazes lost." *

I mean not, however, to condemn, indiscriminately, all metaphysical researches of this kind. It is natural for men of a speculative turn, to extend their views of theology beyond the clear limits either of reason, or of revelation: And if their inquiries be conducted with that humility and reverence, which such subjects should inspire, they may tend to invigorate the understanding, without depraving the heart. The example of Locke, Newton, Clarke, Hartley, and other distinguished philosophers, affords sufficient confirmation of this truth; and at the same time evinces a still more pleasing and important one, that Religion numbers, amongst her votaries, men who have dignified and adorned

* Milton's Paradise Lost, B. II. p 550.

I

human

human nature, by their genius, virtue, and learning. I would particularly recommend to your notice, Sophron, I need not fay to your imitation, the conduct of Mr. Boyle; who had fo profound a veneration for the Deity, that the name of God was never mentioned by him, without a paufe in his difcourfe.* This great philofopher, alfo, had fuch delicate notions of veracity, and was fo fenfible of the imperfection of human knowledge, even when derived from experiment, that in the Preface to his Effays, he makes an apology for the frequent ufe of the words *perhaps, it feems, 'tis not improbable,* as implying a diffidence of the juftnefs of his opinions: And this diffidence arofe, as he informs us, from repeated obfervation, that what pleafed him for a while, was afterwards difgraced by fome further, or more recent difcovery.

Here Philocles was interrupted by the arrival of a ftranger; whofe prefence put an end to the converfation.

* Britifh Biography, Vol. V. p. 248.

O N

ON THE

INFLUENCE

OF

HABIT AND ASSOCIATION.

---------- VIRESQUE ACQUIRIT EUNDO.

VIRGIL.

----------------------- ANGIT,
IRRITAT, MULCET, FALSIS TERRORIBUS
IMPLET.

Hor. Ep. I. Lib. II.

MISCELLANEOUS

OBSERVATIONS

on the INFLUENCE of

HABIT and ASSOCIATION.

SECTION I.

THE laws of HABIT and ASSO-
CIATION form a moſt important
branch both of phyſiology, and of ethics.
And, as *the proper ſtudy of mankind is man*,
every faĉt muſt be deemed intereſting,
which tends to elucidate either the animal, intellectual, or moral œconomy
of his nature. The following obſervations have a reference to one or other
of theſe objects. But no particular regard has been paid to ſyſtem in the

 arrange-

arrangement of them: And I have attempted only, as lord Verulam expresses it, " to write certain brief notes, " set down rather significantly, than " curiously."

I. MUSCULAR ACTIONS, perfectly spontaneous, may be excited without apparent volition, so as to become completely automatic, by the recurrence of those impressions, with which they have been long associated. I shall give a striking example of the truth of this proposition.

Several years ago, the countess of ——— fell into an apoplexy, about seven o'clock in the morning. Amongst other stimulating applications, I directed a feather, dipped in hartshorn, to be frequently introduced into her nostrils. Her ladyship, when in health, was much addicted to the taking of snuff; and the present irritation of the olfactory nerves produced

duced

duced a junction of the fore-finger and thumb, of the right hand; the elevation of them to the nose; and the action of snuffing in the nostrils. When the snuffing ceased, the hand and arm dropped down in a torpid state. A fresh application of the stimulus renewed these successive efforts; and I was a witness to their repetition, till the hartshorn lost its power of irritation, probably by destroying the sensibility of the olfactory nerves. The countess recovered from the fit, about six o'clock in the evening; but, though it was neither long nor severe, her memory never afterwards furnished the least trace of *consciousness* during its continuance.

Does not this instance of a complex series of actions, ordinarily spontaneous, in circumstances which seem to preclude both volition and consciousness, reflect some light on the obscure question, concerning the sleep of the soul, so much

I 4

agitated

agitated in the time of **Mr. Locke**? Is not the opinion of this celebrated philo-sopher confirmed by it, that the perception or contemplation of ideas is to the mind, what motion is to the body, not its essence, but one of its operations: And that an unceasing energy of the under-standing and the will, is the sole prerogative of that infinitely perfect Being, who, according to the language of the Psalmist, *never slumbers or sleeps?*

II. Slight PARALYTIC AFFECTIONS of the organs of speech, sometimes occur, without any correspondent disorder in other parts of the body. In such cases, the tongue appears to the patient too large for his mouth, the saliva flows more copiously than usual, and the vibratory power of the *glottis* is somewhat impaired. Hence, the effort to speak succeeds the volition of the mind, slowly and imperfectly; and the words are uttered with faultering and hesitation. These

Thefe are facts of common notoriety:
But I have never feen it remarked, that
in this local palfy, the pronunciation of
PROPER NAMES is attended with peculiar
difficulty; and that the recollection of
them becomes either very obfcure, or
entirely obliterated; whilft that of perfons, places, things, and even of abftract
ideas, remains unchanged. Such a partial
defect of memory, of which experience
has furnifhed me with feveral examples,
confirms the theory of affociation, and
at the fame time admits of an eafy folution by it. For, as words are arbitrary
marks, and owe their connection with
what they import to eftablifhed ufage;
the ftrength of this connection will be
exactly proportioned to the frequency of
their recurrence; and this recurrence
muft be much more frequent with ge-
neric, than with fpecific terms. Now,
proper names are of the latter clafs; and
the idea of a perfon or place may remain
vivid in the mind, without the leaft

fignature

fignature of the appellative, which dif-
tinguifhes each of them. It is certain,
alfo, that we often think in words; and
there is, probably, at fuch times, fome
flight impulfe on the organs of fpeech,
analogous to what is perceived, when a
mufical note or tune is called to mind.
But a lefion of the power of utterance
may break a link in the chain of affociation, and thus add to the partial defect
of memory, now under confideration.

III. Dr. Willis relates the ftory of
an IDEOT, who, refiding within the found
of a clock, regularly amufed himfelf
with counting aloud the hour of the day,
whenever the hammer of that inftrument
ftruck : But being afterwards removed
to a fituation, where there was no clock,
he ftill retained the former impreffions
fo ftrongly, that he continued to dif-
tinguifh the ordinary divifions of time,
repeating at the end of every hour, the
precife number of ftrokes, which the

clock

clock would have ftruck at that period.* Mr. Addifon has quoted this fact, in one of the Spectators, not from the original, but from Dr. Plott's Hiftory of Stafford-fhire; and has deduced from it many important moral reflections. Whatever may be thought of the authenticity of this narrative, an inftance has lately occurred, within the circle of my own obfervation, fomewhat fimilar, and which no lefs clearly evinces the power of habit to renew former mechanical impreffions, independently of any external caufe.

Mr. W—— had been long confined to his chamber, by a palfy, and other ailments. Every evening, about fix o'clock, he played at cards with fome of the family. He was feized, in June 1780, at three o'clock in the afternoon, with a fit, which terminated in de-fipiency. At the ftated hour of card

* Willis *De Anima Brutor.* Pars I. Cap. xvi. pag. 85.

playing,

playing, he fancied himself to be engaged in his usual game; talked of the cards, as if they were in his hand; and was very angry at his daughter, when she endeavoured to rectify his mistaken imagination. His fatuity was of short continuance; but when recovered from it, he expressed no recollection of what had passed.

IV. A celebrated French writer has remarked, that " the greater degree of " sagacity any one is master of, the more " ORIGINALS will he discover in the " characters of mankind." * This *originality* may doubtless depend on the primary constitution of the mind; but I am persuaded also, that it is often the result of particular associations. When these are unnatural or inordinate, they produce partial alienations of the understanding: And to this source we may trace the visions of enthusiasm, the perse-

* Paschal.

cuting

cuting zeal of bigotry, the fanguinary honour of duelling, the 'fordid purfuits of avarice, and the toilfome folicitudes of ill-directed ambition. Thefe and numberlefs other quixotifms of the mind give the phantoms of imagination an afcendancy over reafon, and produce a temporary infanity, varying according to its object, degree, and duration. If the predominant train of ideas be foreign to the offices of life, there will be little chance of breaking the magic combination; and the habitual indulgence of this tyranny of paffion, or fancy, will, at laft, render it fixed and uncontrolable.

The lunatic, the lover, and the poet,
Are of imagination all compact.
One fees more devils than vaft hell can hold,
That is the madman: The lover, all as frantic,
Sees Helen's beauty on a brow of Egypt:
The poet's eye, in a fine phrenzy rolling,
Doth glance from heaven to earth, from earth to
      heaven;

And

And as imagination bodies forth
The forms of things unknown, the poet's pen
Turns them to shapes, and gives to airy nothing
A local habitation and a name.

SHAKESPEAR.

But, as Horatio fays to Hamlet, "perhaps it may be reasoning too curiously, to reason thus." At least, we should restrict our conclusions, that they may not involve so large a portion of mankind, as to injure the honour even of human nature itself. Besides, passion is the spring of the mind, which gives vigour and energy to all its movements: And, if not extravagantly disproportionate to the value of its object, it may be indulged, not only with innocence, but sometimes even with singular advantage. For, the ardour inspired by it is the source of all that is excellent in genius, and sublime in conduct: And without the salutary aid of this species of enthusiasm, we should sink into a state of torpid apathy.

But

But, though it be difficult to define the precife boundaries of rationality, it can neither be denied, nor concealed, that partial infanity may fubfift with general intelligence; of which the affecting cafe of Mr. Simon Browne affords a curious example. He was a diffenting clergyman, of exemplary life, and eminent intellectual abilities; but having been feized with melancholy, he defifted from the duties of his function, and could not be perfuaded to join in any act, either of public or of private worfhip. The reafon which, after much importunity, he affigned, for this change in his conduct, was, " that he had fallen " under the difpleafure of God, who " had caufed his rational foul gradually " to perifh, and left him only an ani-" mal life, in common with brutes : " that it was therefore profane in him " to pray, and improper to be prefent " at the prayers of others." In this

opinion

opinion he remained inflexible, at the time when all the powers of his mind feemed to fubfift in full vigour; when his judgment was clear, and his reafoning ftrong and conclufive. For at this period he publifhed a defence of the *Religion* of *Nature*, and of the *Chriftian Revelation*, in anfwer to *Tindal's Chriftianity as old as the Creation*: and the work is univerfally allowed to be the beft, which that celebrated controverfy produced. But in a dedication of it to queen Caroline, which fome of his friends found means to fupprefs, he difplays the very extraordinary phrenzy, under which he laboured. Speaking of himfelf, he informs her majefty, " that " by the immediate hand of an aveng- " ing God, his very thinking fubftance " has, for more than feven years, been " continually wafting away, till it is " wholly perifhed out of him, if it be " not utterly come to nothing."

This

This remarkable, and humiliating example of vigour and imbecility, rectitude and perversion of the same understanding, I have related on the authority of Dr. Hawkesworth,* who has preserved the entire copy of the dedication, from which only a brief extract is here made. Our ignorance of the history of Mr. Browne renders it impossible to trace, to its source, this mental malady. But there is reason to presume, that it originated from some strong impression, and subsequent invincible association, connected with, or perhaps producing a change in the organization of the brain. Perhaps, after having acquired an early predilection for the writings of Plato, he might afterwards, in some season of hypochondriacal dejection, fall into the gloomy mysticism of the later followers of that amiable philosopher: For Plotinus, who flourished in the third century

* See the Adventurer.

K   after

after the Chriftian æra, taught that the moft perfect worfhip of the Deity confifts, not in acts of veneration, or of gratitude, but in a certain felf-annihilation, or total extinction of the intellectual faculties.*

I am inclined to believe, that the celebrated M. Pafchal laboured under a fpecies of infanity, towards the conclufion of his life, fimilar to that of Mr. Simon Browne. And, having hazarded fuch a furmife, it is incumbent on me to fhew, on what it is founded. This very extraordinary man difcovered the moft aftonifhing marks of genius in his childhood; and his progrefs in fcience was fo rapid, that at the age of fixteen, he wrote an excellent treatife of Conic Sections. He poffeffed fuch a capacious and retentive memory, that he is faid " never to have forgotten any thing which

* See Collier's Hift. Dict. Alfo Maclaurin's Account of Sir Ifaac Newton's Difcoveries, page 397.

he

he had learned." And it was his practice, to digeft and arrange in his mind, a whole feries of reflections, before he committed them to writing. This power was at once fo accurate and extenfive, that he has been heard to deliver the entire plan of a work, of which he had taken no notes, in a continued narration, that occupied feveral hours. But it is related, by the editor of his *Thoughts on Religion and other Subjects,** " that it pleafed GOD fo to touch his " heart, as to let him perfectly under- " ftand, that the Chriftian religion " obligeth us to live for GOD only, and " to propofe to ourfelves no other " object." In confequence of this perfuafion, he renounced all the purfuits of knowledge, and practifed the moft fevere and rigorous mortifications; living in the greateft penury, and refufing every indulgence, which was not abfolutely

* See the Preface to that work.

K 2 neceffary

neceſſary for the ſupport of life. It appears from ſome of his pious meditations, that this reſolution of mind proceeded from the viſitation of ſickneſs. And the following ſolemn addreſſes to the Deity clearly indicate an imagination perverted by the moſt erroneous aſſociations.

"O Lord, thou gaveſt me health to "be ſpent in ſerving thee, and I applied "it to an uſe altogether profane. Now "thou haſt ſent ſickneſs for my correc- "tion.—I know, O Lord, that at the "inſtant of my death, I ſhall find my- "ſelf entirely ſeparated from the world, "ſtripped naked of all things, ſtanding "alone before thee, to anſwer to thy "juſtice concerning all the motions of "my thoughts, and ſpirits. Grant that "I may look on myſelf as dead already, "ſeparated from the world, ſtripped of "all the objects of my paſſion, and "placed alone in thy preſence.—I praiſe
"thee,

" thee, O God, that thou haſt been
" pleaſed to anticipate the dreadful day,
" by already deſtroying all things to my
" taſte and thoughts, under this weak-
" neſs, which I ſuffer from thy provi-
" dence. I praiſe thee, that thou haſt
" given me this divorce from the plea-
" ſures of the world." Was it conſonant with ſoundneſs of underſtanding, for a man to take a ſudden diſguſt at all the liberal ſtudies, and innocent enjoyments, which had before engaged and gratified his mind? And was it not as much the fiction of a diſtempered fancy, that God enjoined poverty, abſtinence, and ignorance, to one poſſeſſing rank, fortune, and the nobleſt endowments of the mind, as the belief of Simon Browne, that he was diveſted of that rationality, which at the ſame time he ſo eminently diſplayed? Whenever falſe ideas, of a practical kind, are ſo firmly united, as to be conſtantly, and invariably miſtaken for truths, we

K 3   very

very juftly denominate this unnatural alliance INSANITY. And, if it give rife to a train of fubordinate wrong affociations, producing incongruity of behaviour, incapacity for the common duties of life, or unconfcious deviations from morality and religion, MADNESS has then its commencement.

In the foregoing examples, the force of habit and affociation is clearly manifeft. And man, whilft under the influence of their authority, however defpotic or perverted, ftill retains a capacity for action and enjoyment, though he ceafes to be a rational or moral agent. But the fufpenfion of their operation ftops at once all the movements of the mind, and feems to annihilate every energy of the underftanding, the affections, and the will. On the 25th of October 1778, a fea-faring perfon, about forty years of age, was recommended as a patient to the LUNATIC ASYLUM in York.

York.* During his abode in the hof-
pital, he was never obferved to exprefs
any defire for fuftenance, or to fhew any
preference of it to his medicines. The
firft fix weeks after his admiffion, he was
fed in the manner of an infant. A fervant undreffed him at night, and dreffed
him in the morning; after which, he
was conducted to his feat in the common
parlour, where he remained all day, with
his body bent, and his eyes fixed upon
the ground. Every thing was indifferent
to him, and he was regarded by all about
him, as an animal converted nearly into
a vegetable. In this ftate of infenfibility
he remained five years and fix months.
But, on the 14th of May 1782, on his
entrance into the parlour, he faluted the
convalefcents with the words *Good morrow
to you all.* He then thanked the fervants
of the houfe, in the moft affectionate

* This cafe was lately tranfmitted to me, by my friend
Dr. Hunter of York, to be communicated to the Literary
and Philofophical Society of Manchefter. I have given only
an abridgment of it.

K 4

manner,

manner, for their tendernefs to him, of which he had begun to be fenfible fome weeks before, but till then, had not refolution to exprefs his gratitude. A few days after this unexpected recovery, he was permitted to write a letter to his wife, in which he expreffed himfelf with becoming propriety. At this time, he feemed to take peculiar pleafure in the enjoyment of the open air, and in his walks converfed with freedom and fe- renity. On making enquiry concerning what he felt, during the fufpenfion of his intellectual and fenfitive powers, he replied, that his mind had been *totally loft*; but that, about two months before his full reftoration to himfelf, he began to have thoughts and fenfations, which, at firft, ferved only to excite in him fears and apprehenfions, efpecially in the night-time. On the 28th of May 1782, he returned to his family; and has now the command of a fhip employed in the Baltic trade.

SECTION

SECTION II.

I. IT is highly inſtructive, as well as curious, to contemplate the progreſſive influence of particular aſſociations on the affections and the judgment, as they gradually acquire the force of habit by time, and vividneſs by frequent renewal. Dr. Swift, in a letter to lord Bolingbroke, dated 1729, expreſſes himſelf in the following terms. "I remem-"ber, when I was a little boy, I felt "a great fiſh at the end of my line, "which I drew up almoſt on the ground, "but it dropt in, and the diſappointment "vexes me to this very day, and, I be-"lieve, it was the type of all my future "diſappointments."

This little incident, perhaps, gave the firſt wrong bias to a mind, prediſpoſed

to

to fuch impreffions; and by operating with fo much ftrength and permanency, it might poffibly lay the foundation of the Dean's fubfequent peevifhnefs, paffion, mifanthropy, and final infanity. The quicknefs of his fenfibility furnifhed a fting to the flighteft difappointment; and pride feftered thofe wounds, which felf-government would inftantly have healed. As children couple hobgoblins with dark-nefs, every contradiction of his humour, every obftacle to his preferment, was, by him, affociated with ideas of malignity and evil. By degrees, he acquired a con-tempt of human nature, and a hatred of mankind, which, at laft, terminated in the total abolition of his rational faculties.

This is no exaggerated picture, and we have the Dean's own authority for its accuracy. " The chief end," fays he, in a letter to Mr. Pope, " I propofe to " myfelf in all my labours, is to vex " the world, rather than divert it; and,

" if

" if I could compass that design, without
" hurting my own person or fortune, I
" would be the most indefatigable writer
" you have ever seen. I have ever hated
" all nations, professions, and communi-
" ties; and all my love is towards indi-
" viduals. For instance, I hate the tribe
" of lawyers, but I love Counsellor such
" a one, and Judge such a one : 'Tis so
" with physicians, (I will not speak of my
" own trade) soldiers, English, Scotch,
" French, and the rest. But principally
" I hate and detest that animal called
" man, although I heartily love John,
" Peter, Thomas, and so forth. This is
" the system upon which I have governed
" myself many years, (but do not tell)
" and so I shall go on, till I have done
" with them."*

This letter is not written in a strain,
which will suffer the most indulgent

* Pope's Works, Vol. IX. Lett. 2.

critic

critic to afcribe it to jocularity. And in the epitaph, which the Dean compofed for himfelf long afterwards, and which is infcribed on his monument in the cathedral of St. Patrick's, he has left a folemn, and decifive memorial of his mifanthropy.

HIC DEPOSITUM EST CORPUS

JONATHAN SWIFT, S. T. P.

UBI SÆVA INDIGNATIO

ULTERIUS COR LACERARE NEQUIT,

&c.

The ftrongeft tint, in the complexion of the human character, may be sometimes formed by a circumftance, or event apparently cafual; which, by forcibly impreffing the mind, produces a lafting affociation, that gives an uniform direction to the efforts of the underftanding, and the feelings of the heart.

Dr. Conyers Middleton, one of the moft learned, various, and elegant writers

ters of the prefent age, is faid to have been much more addicted, in the early part of his life, to mufic, than to fcience. But he was roufed from his favourite amufement, and ftimulated to the clofeft application to ftudy, by a farcafm of his rival and enemy, the celebrated Dr. Bentley, who ftigmatized him with the name of fidler. *   And indignation made him eager to convince the Doctor and the world, that he could *write* as well as *fiddle* ; a conviction, of which his opponent had, afterwards, the moft painful experience. †

The author of the *Night Thoughts*, a poem which contains the tendereft touches of nature and paffion, and the fublimeft truths of morality and religion, intermixed with frivolous conceits, turgid obfcurities, and gloomy views of human life, wrote that work under the

* Gent. Mag. 1773, page 387.
† Brit. Biograph. Vol. IX.

recent

recent preffure of forrow, for the lofs of his wife, and of a fon and daughter-in-law, whom he loved with paternal tendernefs.   Thefe feveral events happened within the fhort period of three months, as appears from the following apoftrophe to death.

Infatiate archer! could not *one* fuffice?
Thy fhaft flew *thrice*; and *thrice* my peace was flain;
And *thrice*, e'er *thrice* yon moon had fill'd her horns.[*]

But, though time alleviated this diftrefs, his mind acquired from it a tincture of melancholy, which continued through life; and caft a fable hue even on his very amufements.   The like difpofition, alfo, difcovered itfelf in his rural improvements.   He had an alcove in his garden, fo painted as to feem, at a diftance, furnifhed with a bench or feat, which invited to repofe; and when, upon

* Night Thoughts.

a nearer

`a nearer approach, the deception was per-
ceived, this motto at the same time pre-
sented itself to the eye,

Invisibilia non decipiunt.
The things unseen do not deceive us.*

The following witty allusion bears the
marks of a similar turn of thought. The
Doctor paid a visit to Archbishop Potter's
son, then Rector of Chiddingstone, near
Tunbridge. This gentleman lived in
a country, where the roads were deep
and miry; and when Dr. Young, after
some danger and difficulty, arrived at
his house, he enquired, " Whose field is
that which I have crossed ?" " It is
mine," answered his friend. " True,"
said the Poet, " *Potter's field, to bury
strangers in.*" †

* Brit. Biograph. Vol. IX.

† Vid. Gent. Mag. July 1781, page 319.

II. It

II. It is a very important office of education to guard the underſtanding againſt the union of ideas, which have no natural or proper connection. Yet this object is leſs attended to than any other; and we often find men diſtinguiſhed for genius, erudition, and even ſtrength of mind, warped by the falſe conceptions, and governed by the prejudices of puerility. Creduloufneſs is the concomitant of the firſt ſtages of life; and is indeed the principle on which all inſtruction muſt be founded: But it lays the mind open to impreſſions of error, as well as of truth: And, when ſuffered to combine itſelf with that paſſion for the marvellous, which all children diſcover, it foſters the rankeſt weeds of chimera and ſuperſtition; rooting firmly in the mind, *all that the nurſe, and all the prieſt have taught.* Hence, the awful ſolemnity of *darkneſs viſible,* and of what the Poet has denominated *a dim religious light;* together with the terrors of evil

omens,

omens, of haunted places, and of ghaftly fpectres.   The energy and beauty of the following lines depend on the univerfal prevalence of thefe early acquired ideas.

I am thy father's fpirit;
Doom'd for a certain term to walk the night,
And for the day confin'd to faft in fires ;
Till the foul crimes, done in my days of nature,
Are burnt and purg'd away. But, that I am forbid
To tell the fecrets of my prifon houfe,
I could a tale unfold, whofe lighteft word
Would harrow up thy foul, freeze thy young
          blood,
Make thy two eyes, like ftars, ftart from their
          fpheres,
Thy knotty and combined locks to part,
And each particular hair to ftand on end,
Like quills upon the fretful porcupine :
But this eternal blazon muft not be
To ears of flefh and blood. *

Hiftory prefents us with few characters fuperior to thofe of Henry the fourth, of France, and his prime minifter the duke

* Shakefpear's Hamlet.

L   of

of Sully. But notwithstanding the wisdom, knowledge, and discernment of these great men, they appear, on several occasions, to have been actuated, by their juvenile associations, in favour of astrology. What can be more foreign to the events of human life; what less adapted to excite fear or hope in the mind of an intelligent man, than the aspect of a distant star, or the variegated lines of his hand? Yet Sully confesses, that an early prepossession had made him weak enough to give credit to predictions, derived from this fanciful origin. And though he informs us that the king, his master, was of opinion, religion ought to inspire a contempt of such prophecies, the conversation which he relates, at the same time, evidently betrays Henry's confidence in them. This matter is put beyond dispute by an incident, which occurred soon after the birth of the Dauphin; the particulars of which I

shall

fhall recite, from the memoirs of this excellent writer.

* " La Riviere was the king's firſt phy-
" fician, a man who had little more
" religion than thoſe generally poſſeſs,
" who blend it with judicial aſtrology.
" Henry already felt a tenderneſs for
" his ſon, which filled him with an
" eager anxiety to know his fate : And
" having heard that La Riviere ſuc-
" ceeded wonderfully in his predictions,
" he commanded him to calculate the
" Dauphin's nativity, with all the cere-

---

* It ſhould ſeem that aſtrology was conſidered, formerly, as an eſſential part of the learning of a phyſician; for Chaucer, in the prologue to his Canterbury tales, has thus characteriſed him.

> With us there was a doctor of phyſik,
> In al the worlde was ther non hym lyk,
> To ſpeke of phyſik and of ſurgerye ;
> For he was groundit in aſtronomy.
> He kept his pacient a ful gret del
> In hourys by his magyk naturel ;
> Wel couth he fortunen the aſcendent
> Of his ymagys for his pacient.

monials

" monials of art. To aid this bufinefs,
" he had carefully fought for the moft
" accurate watch, which could be pro-
" cured; that the precife moment of
" the prince's birth might be exactly
" afcertained. About a fortnight after-
" wards, the king and Sully being alone
" together, their converfation turned
" upon the prediction of the aftrologer,
" La Broffe, concerning his majefty.
" This renewed Henry's folicitude, with
" refpect to his fon; and he ordered
" La Riviere to be called. ' Monfieur
" La Riviere,' faid the king, ' what
" have you difcovered, relative to the
" Dauphin's deftiny.' ' I had begun my
" calculations,' replied Riviere, ' but
" I left them unfinifhed, not caring to
" amufe myfelf any longer with a fcience,
" which I have always believed to be,
" in fome degree, criminal.' The king,
" diffatisfied with this anfwer, com-
" manded his phyfician to fpeak freely,
" and without concealment, on pain of
" his

" his difpleafure.   La Riviere fuffered
" himfelf to be preffed ftill longer; but
" at laft, with an air of apparent dif-
" content, he delivered himfelf in the
" following terms.   ' Sire, your fon will
" complete the common period of human
" life, and will reign longer than you
" fhall do: But his turn of mind will
" be widely different from yours; he
" will be obftinate in opinion, often
" governed by his own whims, and
" fometimes by thofe of others.   Under
" his adminiftration it will be fafer to
" think, than to fpeak.   Impending
" ruin threatens your former fociety.
" He will perform great exploits, be
" fortunate in his defigns, and make a
" diftinguifhed figure in Europe.   There
" will be a viciffitude of peace and war
" in his time.   He will have children,
" and after his death affairs will grow
" worfe and worfe.   This is all you
" can know from me,' concluded La
" Riviere, ' and more than I had re-

L 3

" folved

" folved to tell you.'   His majefty, and
" the duke of Sully, remained a long
" time together, making reflections on
" the words of the aftrologer, which left
" a ftrong impreffion on the mind of the
" king."

III. Ludicrous associations, not
founded in truth or nature, are peculiarly unfavourable to the principles and
practice of virtue and religion.   Reafon,
efpecially during the period of youth,
affords but a feeble barrier againft the
attacks of ridicule; and the mind that is
enflaved by its influence, may be fo far
deluded or depraved, as to lofe the fuf-
ceptibility of good impreffions, or to
contemplate the moft amiable moral affections with derifion, fhame, and even
difguft.

- - - - - - - - - - - - - - - - Here fubdued
By frontlefs laughter, and the hardy fcorn
Of old, unfeeling vice, the abject foul
With blufhes half refigns the candid praife

Of temperance, and honour; half difowns
A free man's hatred of tyrannic pride;
And hears with fickly fmiles the venal mouth,
With foulest licence, mock the patriot's name.*

The celebrated Dr. Pitcairn was no lefs diftinguifhed for wit than learning. It is recorded, that, as he paffed one day along the ftreets, he beheld the affecting fpectacle of a mafon, killed by the fall, and buried in the ruins, of a chimney, which he had juft completed. " Bleffed are the dead, who die in the Lord," faid he, " for they reft from their labours, and their works follow them." Such a humourous conjunction of refembling yet incongruous ideas, probably ftifled, in his breaft, the fentiments of compaffion. And I have been informed by a very humane friend, that on the relation of a melancholy event, fimilar in its circumftances, the recollection of this ludicrous remark fubftituted, in his mind,

* Akenfide's Pleafures of Imagination, Book III.

L 4

emotions

emotions of laughter, for thofe of com-
miferation.

The natural propenfity of Dean Swift
led him to the indulgence of this fpecies
of drollery, very much to the prejudice
of every finer feeling of the heart. In
one of his letters, he laments the mortal
illnefs of his amiable friend Arbuthnot;
but mixes, with his expreffions of forrow,
certain whimfical reflections, which convert his mourning into grimace. "There
is a paffage in Bede," fays he to Mr.
Pope. "highly commending the piety
" and learning of the Irifh, in that age;
" where, after abundance of praifes, he
" overthrows them all, by lamenting,
" that, alas! they kept Eafter at a wrong
" time of the year. So our Doctor has
" every quality and virtue, that can make
" a man amiable or ufeful; but, *alas!*
" he hath *a fort of flouch in his walk.* I
" pray God protect him, for he is an
" excellent

" excellent Chriftian, though not a ca-
" tholic." *

When the mind has been long habitu-
ated to the affemblage of ludicrous ideas,
they recur on very improper occafions,
not only fpontaneoufly, but even in de-
fpite of every effort of the judgment
and the will. In this ftate, elevation of
thought, and dignity of character, are
unattainable; and ferioufnefs, when af-
fumed, is always marked with fome
glaring and rifible inconfiftency. Swift,
in his laft teftament, bequeaths three
old hats, and other ftill more trifling
and abfurd legacies, with farcical folemnity; and the celebrated Hogarth could
not help difplaying traits of humour, in
his graveft hiftorical paintings. I have
heard it remarked by one, who was
fometimes the companion of his walks,
that he would interrupt the moft interefting converfation, to laugh at any oddity,

* Pope's Works, Vol. IX. Lett. 11.

which

which prefented itfelf; and that his eyes were conftantly caft about, in fearch of objects fingular and diverting. When a man, of this turn, applies himfelf to books, it is not inftruction or rational criticifm, but hilarity, that is his purfuit: And he finds food for his prevailing appetite, equally palatable, both in the beauties and the blemifhes of his author. For Tully has well obferved, that the *verbum ardens*, the glowing boldnefs of expreffion, which fublimity of fentiment infpires, may be eafily rendered ludicrous, by an illiberal paraphrafe. Even entire productions, of fome of the beft writers, have been thus mifreprefented and deformed, for the purpofe of merriment, under the title of travefties. And the bulk of mankind are readily deceived into the belief, that what gives rife to laughter is in itfelf ridiculous. For this reafon, a reader of fenfibility, who has the intereft of virtue and religion at heart, will perufe, with pain and difguft, the

Meditations

*Meditations on a Broom-ſtick, written according to the ſtile and manner of the Honourable Robert Boyle.** " To what a " height," ſays lord Orrery, " muſt the " ſpirit of ſarcaſm ariſe in an author, " who could prevail upon himſelf to "ridicule ſuch a man as Mr. Boyle ! " But the ſword of wit, like the ſcythe " of time, cuts down friend and foe, and " attacks every thing that accidentally " lies in its way." It muſt be confeſſed, however, that this great and good philoſopher has indulged, in his theological writings, certain conceits, which will draw a ſmile from his warmeſt admirers. A zeal to promote the habit of pious and moral reflections has, ſometimes, tempted him to force ideas into the moſt unnatural alliance ; and to deduce very important analogies, from objects or circumſtances, not only incongruous, but low and contemptible. Thus, from the

* Swift's Works, Vol. V. p. 372.

ſtumbling

ftumbling of a horfe, in a good road, he infers the danger of profperity; from being let blood in a fever, he juftifies the wifdom of the Deity, in depriving his creatures of fpiritual fuperfluities; and from a diftafte of the fyrups, prefcribed by his phyfician, he concludes, that the good things of life are not objects of envy, becaufe not always relifhed as enjoyments. But I feel a reluctance to point out fuch trivial exuberances, in the works of Mr. Boyle. It is ungenerous to injure the well earned wreath of laurel, which he wears, by faftidioufly culling a few folitary leaves, that are withered. We fhould remember alfo, that dignity and meannefs, grace and vulgarity, have, in many inftances, no fixed ftandard; and are dependent on certain acceffory affociations, which vary in different countries, at different periods of time, and with different perfons even of the fame age and place. Jacob is reprefented, in the holy Scriptures, as

calling

calling his sons together, before his death, to deliver to each of them his benediction. And in the language of metaphor and prophecy, he says, *Issachar is a strong ass, couching down between two burdens:* From which it appears, that this animal was not then regarded as a symbol of stupidity and insignificance. Ajax, retreating between two armies, is compared, by Homer, to the lion for undaunted courage, and to the ass for sullen and unyielding slowness.* But Mr. Pope, in his translation, has omitted the latter allusion, to accommodate his work to the state of modern opinion. The same sublime poet exhibits the awful uncertainty of victory, in the engagement between the Greeks and Trojans, by the image of a poor woman, weighing wool in a pair of scales. And Eustathius says, it was a tradition, that Homer derived this simile from the occupation of his mother, who main-

* Il. Lib. XI.

tained

tained herfelf by fuch manual labour.*
But a ftill more remarkable comparifon
occurs, in the writings of this ancient
bard. For Ulyffes, toffing about through
the whole night, with reftlefs anxiety, is
likened to a fat pudding, frying on the
fire.†   Even Virgil, whofe elegance and
correctnefs are univerfally acknowledged,
has drawn the fimilitude of a queen
(Amata the wife of king Latinus) under
the violence of paffion, from a company
of boys whipping a top.‡

I do not recollect one coarfe allufion,
or low image in the whole poem of
Paradife Loft; though feveral, contained
in it, are fantaftical, being derived from
the fictions of heathen mythology. But
it is more than probable that Milton,
when tranflated by foreigners, will not
appear to deferve the character of un-

* See the Notes of Dacier, Pope, and other Commentators.

† Od. Lib. XXI.   ‡ Æn. Lib. VII.

deviating

deviating dignity. For the correspondent terms, in other languages, may have secondary ideas of meanness affixed to them, from which, in the original, they are exempt. The same remark is applicable to other works; and it is particularly to be wished, that the books of the Old and New Testament, in the common version, were always perused with a candid attention to it.

I have been told of a picture, which exhibits a burlesque view of the tablature, representing the judgment of Hercules. The young Hero is painted as a tall grenadier, Virtue as a methodist preacher, and Pleasure as a drunken strumpet. The parody, if this term can be applied to painting, may answer the purpose of exciting laughter, but will counteract, in the spectator's mind, all the beneficial effects of the most instructive and philosophical apologue of antiquity.

Discit

Difcit enim citius, meminitque libentius illud
Quod quis deridet, quam quod probat et veneratur.

                                        HOR.

PARODY is a favourite flower both of ancient and of modern literature.* It is a fpecies of ludicrous compofition, which derives its wit from affociation; and never fails to produce admiration and delight, when it unites tafte in felection, with felicity of application. Even licentious fpecimens of it move to laughter; for we are always inclined to be diverted with mimickry, or ridiculous imitation, whether the original be an object of refpect, of indifference, or of contempt. A polifhed Athenian audience heard, with burfts of mirthful applaufe, the difcourfes of the venerable Socrates, burlefqued upon the ftage; and no Englifhman can read the Rehearfal without fmiling at the medley of borrowed abfurdities, which it exhibits.

* See Diog. Laertius, Lucian. Dialog. Boileau, Cervantes, Butler, Swift, &c. &c.

                                        Mr.

Mr. Pope's *Dunciad, and Rape of the Lock* abound with the most admirable parodies; but some of them may appear, to a religious mind, chargeable with levity and profaneness. I shall quote an example, both of the excellent and exceptionable; as the beauty of the one, and the fault of the other, equally relate to the subject of the present essay.

When the fatal rape was committed by the Baron, on Belinda's Lock, she is represented as attempting to revenge herself by her bodkin.

Now meet thy fate, incens'd Belinda cry'd,
And drew a deadly bodkin from her side.
The same, his ancient personage to deck,
Her great great grandsire wore about his neck,
In three seal rings; which after, melted down,
Formed a vast buckle for his widow's gown :
Her infant grandame's whistle next it grew,
The bells she jingled, and the whistle blew ;
Then in a bodkin graced her mother's hairs,
Which long she wore, and now Belinda wears. *

* Canto V. line 87.

M

The

The unlearned reader will be struck with this splendid, genealogical description of an insignificant bodkin: But he, who is versed in the writings of Homer, will peruse it with additional delight, from the recollection of the analogy, which it bears to the progress of Agamemnon's sceptre. In the third Canto, of the incomparable poem above referred to, a game of Ombre is described with all the *pathos* and solemnity, which the heroic muse can call forth: And the cards in Belinda's hand being pompously enumerated, viz.

---------- Four kings, in majesty rever'd,
With hoary whiskers, and a forky beard:
And four fair queens, whose hands sustain a flow'r,
Th' expressive emblem of their softer power, &c.

the two following lines succeed;

The skilful nymph reviews her force with care,
Let Spades be trumps! she said; and trumps they were.

This parody of one of the most sublime passages in the Old Testament,

" *and*

" *and* God *said, Let there be light, and there was light,*" may, I think, be juſtly deemed reprehenſible ; as it tends to connect a ludicrous idea with that Being, who ought never to be thought of, but with reverence. * But ſhould this remark appear to be an overſtrained refinement, it will be acknowledged that, in leſs

---

* Pope ſeems to have been peculiarly fond of alluſions to this paſſage, of the Old Teſtament ; but has been a little unfortunate in the application of them. The truth is, that the ſentiment is too ſublime, either for burleſque, or for compliment. And the extravagance of theſe lines, in his epitaph on Sir Iſaac Newton, offends almoſt equally with the parody quoted above.

> Nature, and Nature's laws lay hid in night ;
> God *ſaid, Let Newton be !* and all was light.

This hyperbolical encomium is ſuch a profanation of ſacred writ, to monumental flattery, that it was juſtly ſatirized in the following epigram, written by a young man, who has diſcloſed only the initials of his name.

> If Newton's exiſtence enlighten'd the whole,
> What part of expanſion inhabits the fool ?
> If light had been total, as Pope hath averr'd,
> I. T. had been right, for he could not have err'd :
> But Pope has his faults, ſo excuſe a young ſpark ;
> Bright Newton's deceas'd, and we're all in the dark.

M 2

dignified

dignified cafes, very flight affociations, of the burlefque kind, have an aftonifhing effect on the fentiments and tafte of thofe who form them. When Thomfon's tragedy of Sophonifba was firft reprefented on the ftage, the higheft expectations were formed of its theatrical merit. But a waggifh parody on the following line,

  O! Sophonifba! Sophonifba, O!

damned the reputation of the play; and for a while the town echoed with

  O! Jemmy Thomfon! Jemmy Thomfon, O!*

It happened not long fince, that a perfon of mean rank was elected provoft, or chief magiftrate, of Aberdeen. In the firft moments of elevation, and

---

* Johnfon's Lives of the Poets; Article, Thomfon.

This celebrated critic, in another part of the fame work, has well obferved, that exclamations feldom fucceed in our language: And that the particle O! ufed at the beginning of a fentence, always offends.

whilft

whilft receiving the congratulations of his friends, he laid his hands upon his breaft, and very emphatically declared, that " *after all be was but a mortal man.*"

Is it poffible for any one, under the impreffion of this ludicrous ftory, to read, without fmiling, the fact related by Ælian, and quoted with great applaufe by many other hiftorians, viz. that Philip, king of Macedon, kept a perfon in his fervice, whofe office it was to deliver to him, daily, the following admonition; *Remember, Philip, that thou art mortal?* Perhaps, if fuch an incident had occurred in Greece, during the reign of that monarch, it might have turned into ridicule the admiration, in which his inftitution was held; by expofing, at once, the abfurdity, pride, and affected humility, on which it was founded.

The people improperly, becaufe opprobrioufly, called Quakers, certainly merit

a very

a very high degree of efteem from their fellow citizens, on account of their induftry, temperance, peaceablenefs, and catholic fpirit of charity. For notwithftanding the enthufiaftic pretenfions of their founders, to fuperior fanctity and Divine infpiration, they difclaimed all dominion over faith and confcience. And Barclay, their learned apologift, wrote ably in defence of religious liberty; whilft Penn, as a lawgiver and civil magiftrate, eftablifhed it, on the broadeft foundation, in his new government of Penfylvania.* At a period, when bigotry and perfecution were predominant through the Chriftian world, fuch rational

* This venerable man was fufpected of being a papift in difguife, owing to the favour fhewn him by king James II. To obviate fo unjuft an opinion, feveral letters were written by him to Dr. Tillotfon, then dean of Canterbury, who, amongft others, had adopted it; and in one of them he thus expreffes himfelf. "I know not a jefuit or a prieft in the "world: And yet I am a catholic, though not a Roman. "I have bowels for mankind, and dare not deny others, "what I crave for myfelf, I mean, liberty for the exercife of "my

rational fentiments and liberal conduct reflect the higheft honour on this fect. But the fingularity of their apparel, manners, and forms of worfhip, has expofed them to the keeneft fhafts of ridicule. And however illiberally and unjuftifiably fuch offenfive weapons may have been employed, they would, in all probability, have prevailed, if the converts and youth of this fect had not been fortified againft them, by the moft unremitting ftrictnefs of their inftitutions. Thefe are admirably calculated to correct, or to prevent, all ludicrous affociations; and to fupprefs, if poffible, the very principle of laughter, as inconfiftent with the *ferioufnefs, gravity, and*

" my religion; thinking faith, piety, and providence, a better
" fecurity than force; and that, when truth cannot prevail
" with her own weapons, all others will fail her.---I am no
" Roman Catholic, but a Chriftian, whofe creed is the
" Scripture, of the truth of which I hold a nobler evidence,
" than the beft church authority in the world."

Brit. Biog. Vol. VII.

M 4

godly

*godly fear of the Gospel.** It is astonishing to observe, in a large body of people,
the efficacy of a set of practical maxims,
utterly repugnant to nature: And the
influence of them is early visible, even
in their children; who display an invariable steadiness of countenance and deportment, under circumstances which
cover others, of the same age, but differently educated, with the blushes of
bashful confusion. But there is now
an increasing relaxation of discipline
amongst the members of this respectable
community; and their distinguishing
modes will gradually cease, as they become more and more combined with
the painful ideas of obloquy and derision,
in the minds of those who adopt them.

Piety to God, whether it respects the
inward sentiments and affections of the
soul, or the outward expressions of them
in homage and prayer, ought to elevate

* Barclay's Apology for the Quakers, p. 136.

us

us far above the reach of raillery, or the influence of low and ludicrous associations. But unhappily, both the principle and practice of devotion are too often debased by superstition, deformed by enthusiasm, and counterfeited by hypocrisy: And as these constitute legitimate objects of ridicule and contempt, the sterling value of piety itself becomes depreciated by the union of a base and foreign alloy. Such numbers *draw near to the Deity with their lips, whilst their hearts are far from him*, that a noble writer has sarcastically observed, " If we are told a man is reli-
" gious, we still ask, what are his morals?
" But if we hear at first that he has honest
" morals, and is a man of natural justice
" and good temper, we seldom think of
" the other question, whether he be
" religious and devout?" * These are considerations, which operate powerfully on the mind: And if they be strengthened by the ideas of ungraceful gestures,

---

* Lord Shaftsbury's Characteristics.

diffonant

diffonant tones of voice, or other ex-
travagancies in devotion, such a degree
of timidity and false delicacy may be
created, as entirely to deprefs the fervour,
which thefe exercifes are adapted to excite. Prayer may then be performed as
a duty, but will not be felt as a privilege;
and the creature will even blufh at the
higheft honour he can enjoy, that of
holding communion with his Creator.
Many an ingenuous youth has been defpoiled of this glorious diftinction of humanity, by the fneers and jefts of his
companions: And of the military profeffion it is faid, that an officer would
rather face the mouth of a cannon, than
be found privately in the pofture of
fupplication. Dr. Swift feems to have
been governed, in his religious obferv-
ances, by fome fuch ill-grounded affociation. His conftant prefence at church,
whilft he refided at the deanery of St.
Patrick's, he knew would be expected;
but he was feduloufly careful to conceal

whatever

whatever had the appearance of voluntary devotion. When he was in London, therefore, he never attended divine service, but at a very early hour in the morning. And though he practised family prayer in his houfe, his fervants affembled, as it were, by ftealth; fo that Dr. Delany lived fix months with him, before he difcovered it. *

I hope it will not be underftood, from what has been advanced on the topic of ludicrous affociations, that I am averfe to laughter, or an enemy to wit and pleafantry. Human life, without their exhilarating influence, would be a fcene

* Brit. Biog. Vol. VIII.   Johnfon's Lives of the Poets, Article Swift.

Dr. Swift furnifhes an excellent fubject for the moral anatomift. His life was eventful; his paffions were various and ftrong; and his fenfibilities acute in the extreme. Self-indulgence gave every fpring to action, within him, its full power; and pride prevented the concealment of its operation. Hence the motives, which directed his conduct, were feldom either extraneous or complex; and they are generally eafy to be traced to their fource.

of

of anxious care, or phlegmatic dulnefs.
Nor is the harfher controul of ridicule
to be wholly condemned or rejected.   It
is neceffary to reftrain the irregular fallies
of folly; and, as thefe often proceed from
a lively imagination, the fenfe of it is
happily acuteft, where its correction is
moft required.

IV.   There are few people, who have
not, at particular feafons, experienced
the effect of certain accidental affociations, which obtrude one impertinent
idea, or fet of ideas, on the mind, to the
exclufion of every other.   Mr. Locke
has noticed this weaknefs, and he hu-
mouroufly defcribes it, " as a childifhnefs
" of the underftanding, wherein, during
" the fit, it plays with and dandles fome
" infignificant puppet, without any end
" in view."*   Thus, a tune, a proverb,

* Locke's Conduct of the Underftanding.

a fcrap

a scrap of poetry, or some other trivial object, will steal into the thoughts, and continue to possess them long after it ceases to be amusing. Persuasives to dismiss a guest that proves so trouble-some, can hardly be necessary; and bodily exertion is generally the best remedy for this mental infirmity. But there is another state of mind, dependent on the laws of association, which is more dangerous, because it invites to indulgence. It consists in reveries, gay visions of fancy, the creation of air-built castles, and cobweb *hypotheses*. Men of genius alone are incident to these flattering delusions; and they too often implicitly give way to them. But in proportion as they prevail, reason and judgment are impaired; study becomes formal dulness; activity toilsome; and the necessary offices of life are neglected. Thomson has thus beautifully pictured such a character.

There

There was a man of special grave remark ;
A certain tender gloom o'erspread his face,
Pensive, not sad, in thought involv'd, not dark;
As sweet this wight could sing as morning lark,
And teach the noblest morals of the heart :
But these his talents were y' buried stark.

To noon-tide shades incontinent he ran,
Where purls the brook with sleep inviting sound,
There would he linger till the latest ray
Of light sat trembling on the welkin's bound.
Oft as he travers'd the cœrulean field,
And mark'd the clouds, that drove before the
        wind,
Ten thousand glorious systems would he build,
Ten thousand great ideas fill'd his mind ;
But with the clouds they fell, and left no trace
        behind. *

V.   It has been remarked, that game-
sters, sailors, and others, who are under
the influence of what is vulgarly, but
very improperly, termed *chance*, that is,
of causes not within the reach of human
power to direct, nor of human sagacity

* Thomson's Castle of Indolence, Canto I.

to difcern, are extremely prone to fuper-ftition. Their hopes and fears, their confidence and defpair, are founded on circumftances, which bear only a fanciful relation to the events, that are to come. Imagination connects the ideas of magnitude and importance with the flighteft caufes, which are viewed in obfcurity; as objects appear largeft to our fenfes during twilight. A gamefter lays great ftrefs on the luck of a feat, or the fhake of a die: And I remember, in croffing a ferry, whilft it was very calm, the boatman whiftled more than three hours a particular fet of notes, to forward the motion of his veffel, crying out, at fhort intervals, *Blow, good wind, blow; blow a brifk gale!* And if a gentle gale fprung up, he redoubled his efforts, in the fulleft affurance of fuccefs. The abfolute truft, repofed in empirical medicines, arifes from a fimilar deception; and the miraculous operation, often afcribed to them, even by perfons of judgment and education,

education, is a proof of the astonishing power of wrong associations. The wise emperor Marcus Aurelius was so firmly persuaded of the efficacy of a certain antidote, called *theriaca*, to resist every species of poison, that he made use of it daily, to the great injury of his health. For his head became affected to such a degree, that he dozed in the midst of business; and when opium was left out of the composition, an obstinate watchfulness ensued.*

The same principle of association explains the dogmatism of the critic, and the antiquarian; whose positiveness, respecting the construction of a sentence, or the letters of a worn-out inscription, is often in exact proportion to their uncertainty. When any one soars, with great ardour, into the regions of conjecture, the airy phantoms, which he meets with, will be contemplated by

* Galen de Antidotis, Lib. I. C. 1.

him

him as fubftantial realities : And he will purfue truth, not with a temperate and rational zeal, but with the blind enthufiafm of love ; dignifying, like a paffionate *inamorato*, every conceit of his mind, and admiring difcoveries which exift no where, but in his own brain. Thefe reflections have been, in part, fuggefted by the perufal of the memoirs of Mr. Whifton ; a man, whofe genius, learning, and integrity, might have placed him high in the fcale of excellence, had he not fuffered a perverted imagination to ufurp the juft authority of judgment. " The warmth of his temper difpofed " him to receive any fudden thoughts, " any thing, that ftruck his fancy, when " favourable to his preconceived fcheme " of things, or to any new fchemes of " things, which ferved, in his opinion, " a religious purpofe."* With fuch propenfities he wrote *An Effay on the Revelation of St. John :* And being appointed,

* Mr. Collins.

the following year (1707), to preach Mr. Boyle's lectures, he chose for his subject, the *accomplishment of Scripture prophecies.* In 1712, when prince Eugene of Savoy was in England, he dedicated a work to him, in which *he interpreted the end of the hour, and day, and month, and year, for the Ottoman devaſtations, Apoc. 9.15. to have been put by his glorious victory over the Turks, September 1, 1697. O. S. or the ſucceeding peace of Carlowitz, 1698.* His favourite conceptions were now ſo ſtrongly rivetted in his mind, that he diſcerned clearly all the revolutions of paſt and future ages, in the writings of the Prophets, or the revelations of St. John. Such indeed was the aſcendency of theſe abſurd aſſociations over his underſtanding, that he gave entire credit to the impudent impoſture of Mary Tofts,

---

* Prince Eugene ſeems to have been pleaſed with the honour of the diſcovery, that he was the object of ſo ancient a prediction; for he preſented Mr. Whiſton, on this occaſion, with a purſe of gold. See Brit. Biog. Vol. VIII. p. 247.

a woman

a woman of Godalmin, who pretended to be delivered of rabbits, becaufe her monftrous births were deemed, by him, to be the exact completion of an old prediction in Efdras.*

In almoft every cafe of wrong affociations, the underftanding either voluntarily fufpends its controling and directing power, or is deluded into a conformity with fancy; and the mind ftill retains a confcioufnefs of freedom, and of moral agency. But there are certain habits, which ufurp, by *force*, the dominion of reafon, and compel the will to gratify inordinate defires, by the choice of known evil, in preference to acknowledged good. The lamentation of the poet, *video meliora proboque, deteriora fequor*, feems alfo to have been felt by St. Paul, who fays, Rom. vii. 11. *That which I do, I allow not; for what I would, that I do*

* Gent. Mag. July 1781, p. 321.

not;

not; but what I hate, that I do. If then I do that, which I would not, I consent unto the law, that it is good. Now then it is no more I that do, but sin that dwelleth in me. If an enlightened Apostle speaks in such abasing terms of himself, with how much more truth and propriety might the same language have been adopted, by a late advocate for the divine dispensation of the Gospel. For charity inclines me to hope, that the learned author of the Christian Hero *wrote* in consistency with, whilst he *acted* in opposition to, his most serious conviction. This work, Sir Richard Steele informs us,* was composed by him, principally with a view to contrast impressions of piety and virtue, with the strong propensity, which he experienced, to licentious pleasures. For he says, even when rioting in scenes of debauchery, he was deeply conscious of the impropriety of his conduct, and

* See his Apology for himself and his writings.

condemned

condemned thofe unlawful gratifications, which he had not refolution to renounce. His Chriftian Hero, however, whilft the treatife remained privately in his own hands, afforded but a weak and ineffectual check to his vicious purfuits. He, therefore, determined to publifh it; that, by thus placing himfelf in a new light, before his acquaintance, he might be reftrained from guilt, by an explicit and avowed teftimony in favour of goodnefs. But it does not appear that this fingular experiment proved fuccefsful. Steele forfook not his debaucheries; and by having affected the faint, he aggravated, in the opinion of his friends, his condemnation as a finner. Yet, Mr. Pope, who knew him well, juftified him from the imputation of hypocrify; and always regarded him as a real lover of virtue, in *theory*, though a flave to vice, in *practice*.*

---

* Ruffhead's Life of Pope, p. 493. Brit. Biog. Vol. VIII.

N 3

Many

Many other examples might be ad-
duced of the force of evil habits, and
the pernicious influence of falfe affociations, whether intellectual or moral: But
to dwell long on the fhades of the human
character, is apt to abate our benevolence to mankind; and to impair the
principle of veneration, towards the great
Author of our nature.   More pleafing
would be the tafk, and I will add, more
eafy too, to vindicate the wifdom of the
Divine laws, by fhewing, that the power
of habit, and the propenfity to combine
ideas together, are effential to the juft
conftitution of the mind :   And that,
without their well regulated aid, knowledge would be unattainable, virtue a
tranfient emotion or defultory act, and
life itfelf a fcene of indifference and
infipidity,

O N

INCONSISTENCY of EXPECTATION,

I N

LITERARY PURSUITS.

N 4

RETINUIT, QUOD EST DIFFICILLIMUM, EX
SAPIENTIA MODUM.

TACIT. VIT. AGRICOL.

RETINUIT, QUOD EST DIFFICILLIMUM, EX
SAPIENTIA MODUM.

TACIT. VIT. AGRICOL.

INCONSISTENCY of EXPECTATION,

I N

LITERARY PURSUITS.

> He, who hath treafures of his own,
> May leave a cottage, or a throne;
> May quit the world to dwell alone,
> Within his fpacious mind.

WHERE, amongft the men of Science, is the Archetype to be found, of a picture fo flattering to human pride? The original, from which it appears to have been drawn, was, indeed, an exalted character; but at the fame time, alas! a feeble valetudinarian, who muft have experienced thofe mortify-

ing

ing impediments to mental exertion, which arife from a conftitution naturally delicate, and broken by laborious refearches into truth. Under fuch circumftances, could it be affirmed, that

> Locke had a foul,
> Wide as the fea,
> Calm as the night,
> Bright as the day;
> There might his vaft ideas play,
> Nor feel a thought confin'd.

The amiable Poet, * who has thus pourtrayed, with the glowing colours of admiration and refpect, one of the moft diftinguifhed ornaments of the human fpecies, paffed himfelf a life of lingering ficknefs: And, though his genius was fertile, and his induftry wonderfully and varioufly productive, yet, fuch was his fenfibility of the obftructions he had to furmount, that he made a painful and

* Dr. Watts.

humiliating

humiliating calculation of the days, months, and years, which he had loft, even by his flighteft malady, the tooth-ach. The celebrated M. Pafcal languifh-ed, four years, under a diftemper, which, without manifefting itfelf by many out-ward figns, or occafioning confinement, debarred him of the pleafures and im-provements of ftudy. And it was the anxious office of his friends, to guard him from writing, or fpeaking on any topics, which might exercife much thought or attention.* Mr. Pope's vital functions were fo difordered, that his life is emphatically faid to have been a *long difeafe*. The head-ach was his moft frequent affailant; and he ufed to relieve it, by inhaling the fteams of coffee, which he often required during thofe hours, that fhould have afforded the refrefhment of fleep: Such was his earneftnefs and folicitude in the profecu-

* Preface to Pafcal's Thoughts.

tion

tion of his literary undertakings, that Swift complains, he was never at leifure for converfation. And one of lord Oxford's domeftics related, that in the fevere winter of 1740, fhe was called from her bed four times, in one night, to fupply him with paper, that he might not lofe a thought.* The learned biographer, who, with all the feverity of farcafm, records this fact, acknowledges, in the preface to the moft laborious of his works, that he himfelf *triumphed* in the acquifitions, which he fhould difplay to mankind: and indulged all the dreams of a Poet doomed, at laft, to wake a Lexicographer. For he found that " one enquiry only gave occafion " to another, that book referred to " book; that to fearch was not always " to find; and to find was not always " to be informed; and that thus to pur- " fue perfection, was, like the firft in- " habitants of Arcadia, to chace the

* Johnfon's Lives of the Poets.

" fun,

" fun, which, when they had reached
" the hill where he feemed to reft, was
" ftill beheld at the fame diftance from
" them." There is a paffage in Thomfon's *Caftle of Indolence,* fo applicable to
this kind of folly, that I am tempted to
tranfcribe it.

This globe pourtray'd the race of learned men,
Still at their books, and turning o'er the page,
Backwards and forwards: oft they fnatch the pen,
As if infpir'd, and in a Thefpian rage,
Then write and blot, as would your ruth engage.
Why, authors! all this fcrawl and fcribbling fore?
To lofe the prefent, gain the future age,
Praifed to be, when you can hear no more ;
And much enrich'd with fame, when ufelefs
        worldly ftore? *

The examples, which I have recited,
are of men occupied chiefly, if not folely,
in the walks of literature. But the tafte
for knowledge may be cultivated, fuc-
cefsfully, in the bufy fcenes of active

* Thomfon's Caftle of Indolence, Canto I.

life.

life.   And under thefe circumftances, aftonifhing proficiency has been made, by the combined powers of genius and induftry.   The works of Tully, Pliny the elder, Bacon, Temple, and Bolingbroke, not to mention various other names of ancient and modern times, are fufficient evidences of this fact.   But neither the efforts of genius nor of induftry can ward off ficknefs, obviate folicitude, or ftop thofe unaccountable ebbings of the mind, which even a lowering fky will fometimes produce.   Cicero, notwithftanding all his exultation, on the foothing influence of philofophy, found himfelf under the neceffity of retiring, at certain feafons, to one of his country villas, fituated near Aftura. And in this folitary refidence, which was covered with a thick wood, cut into fhady walks, he ufed to pafs his hours of fpleen and melancholy.*

* Middleton's Life of Cicero, Vol. III. p. 296.

But

But could we fuppofe health to be enjoyed without interruption, the fpirits to be always lively and active, and all the intellectual faculties in a ftate of uniform compofure and energy, yet ftill the progrefs in knowledge would be retarded by error, and obftructed by the want of thofe materials, for which we muft depend on the accuracy, induftry, and attainments of others. The temple of fcience requires, for its elevation, the united labours of myriads of different artifts; and the conftruction of it will be perpetually incident to delays, by the indolence, unfkilfulnefs, and miftakes of thofe, who are employed in the undertaking. In fuch circumftances, to unite ardour with ferenity, an enthufiafm for fcience with patience under all the obftructions of purfuit, from outward accident or inward infirmity, is a happinefs, of which few can boaft.* And the page

* Sir Ifaac Newton affords a fingular example of temperate ardour, unremitting energy, and almoft invariable equanimity.

of biography is filled with narratives of the queruloufnefs, impaired health, and mental imbecility of thofe, who, by their writings, have informed, enlightened, and charmed mankind. Juft views of the defigns of Providence, in the government of the world, and particularly in the ftructure of the human mind with refpect to the progreffive evolution of its faculties, would tend to obviate thefe evils, by reftraining the inordinate afpirations of literary ambition, and by correcting the inconfiftency of expectation, from which they proceed.

Man is evidently conftituted for two great ends; the attainment of virtue, and of knowledge. All his mental endowments have a reference to one or other of thefe final caufes: On them, therefore, muft depend the *perfection,* and *felicity* of his nature. But his moral powers feem more circumfcribed in their operation, and confequently to admit of lefs exten-

five

five culture, than thofe of his underftanding. For they are confined within
the limits of rational, or at moft of
fenfitive being, and with fuch they can
hold only a partial, and contracted cor-
refpondence : whilft the intellectual faculties have, for their object, the whole
fyftem of nature, the infinitude of which
is, perhaps, not lefs apparent in its mi-
nutenefs, than immenfity. From thefe
confiderations, I am inclined to believe,
that our ftation, in the prefent world, is
intended for near approaches towards
the *maturity* of *virtue*; but for the *infancy*
only of *knowledge.* And the wifdom of
this ordinance, of the Deity, is fufficiently
difcernible. For as *knowledge* is *power,*
the antecedent poffeffion of goodnefs, to
direct it, muft be effentially neceffary to
beatitude. The paffions and affections
are of fpeedy growth, and often manifeft
great vigour in that feafon of life, which
is marked by the feeblenefs of reafon.
Increafing years modify, direct, and me-

O

liorate

liorate them; but the difcipline of experience ferves rather to balance and
reftrain, than to augment their native
ftrength and energy. On the contrary,
the mind proceeds by flow and regular
gradations, in the attainment of fcience.
And our acquifitions confift not, folely,
in the difcovery of new objects or phæ-
nomena; but in the comparifon of thefe
with what we already know,* and in
afcertaining their reciprocal dependen-
cies, relations, or contrarieties. Thus
knowledge is multiplied beyond the fum
of its feparate and component parts:
And every acceffion to it increafes the
ftock in a ratio, that, we may devoutly
truft, will become greater and greater
through all eternity.

But the bulk of mankind, in this ftage
of exiftence, are in circumftances, which
preclude any confiderable advancement

* Maclaurin's View of Sir Ifaac Newton's Philofophy.

in

in learning. And we may obferve, that the difpenfation of the Gofpel gives no *direct* encouragement to it,* but applies all its precepts and exhortations to the cultivation of the heart. For the principles and practice of virtue are accommodated to every period and condition of life; and are exercifed, refined, and exalted even by poverty, infirmity, ficknefs, and old age; all which check the exertions, and deprefs the vigour of human genius. Rectitude of difpofition and of conduct bears a precife and permanent relation to all times, perfons, and occurrences. And if we afcend from particular to general excellence, by contemplating the duty of man in the aggregate, we may form a diftinct and

---

* Many paffages, in the New Teftament, according to a literal interpretation, feem *directly levelled againft* human learning; which is defcribed as vain, deceitful, traditionary, confifting of endlefs genealogies, idle babblings, and profane fables. But the beft commentators are of opinion, that thefe cenfures have a reference only to the abfurd philofophy of the Gnoftics or Sophifts, which was derived from the Egyptians.

 adequate

adequate idea of *moral perfection*. But what mind can expand itself to the conception of *complete intelligence!*—Every step of our afcent, on the hill of fcience, prefents to the view a widening horizon; and the boundary of darknefs increafes, in proportion to the amplitude of thofe enlightened regions, which it incircles.

It is this endlefs progreffion of knowledge, which is apt to give the *love* of it an inordinate afcendency over every other principle, fo as to render it the *ruling paffion* of the mind. And, as this paffion does not, like the love of virtue, temper its particular exertions, by preferving a due fubordination in the powers which it calls forth into action, the wildeft extravagances, of emotion and of conduct, have been difplayed by thofe, who fubmit to its uncontrouled dominion. A great philofopher has rufhed naked, from the bath,

into

into the ftreets of a populous city, frantic with joy, on the folution of an interefting problem. Tacitus informs us,
that his excellent father-in-law Agricola
" was inclined to have engaged more
" deeply, in the ftudies of philofophy
" and law, than was fuitable to a Roman
" and a fenator, if the difcretion of his
" mother had not reftrained the warmth
" and vehemence of his difpofition:
" For his high fpirit, inflamed by the
" charms of glory and exalted reputa-
" tion, led him to the purfuit, with
" more eagernefs than judgment. Rea-
" fon, and riper years, mitigated his
" ardour; and, what is a *moft difficult tafk,*
" *he preferved moderation in fcience itfelf.*"*
The emperor Marcus Antoninus, in one
of his meditations, expreffes fervent gratitude to the gods, that, by their favour,
he had made no further advances in

* Tacitus in Vit. Agric. See, alfo, Mr. Aikin's elegant
tranflation of this admirable piece of Biography, p. 65.

O 3

rhetoric,

rhetoric, poetry, and other amusing studies; that he had not bestowed too much time on voluminous reading, logical disputations, or researches into physics; because these might have engrossed his mind, or diverted his attention from the peculiar duties of his elevated station.* Just and weighty, therefore, is the maxim of another ancient moralist, with which I shall conclude these reflections, that *we should not rest satisfied with the* WORDS *of wisdom, without the* WORKS; *nor turn philosophy into an idle pleasure, which was given us for a salutary remedy.*†

* Marc. Antonin. Lib. I.   † Seneca.

ADVANTAGES OF A TASTE

BEAUTIES OF NATURE,
AND OF ART.

ME VERO PRIMUM DULCES ANTE OMNIA MUSÆ
ACCIPIANT! ------------
                                        VIRG.

QUID MINUAT CURAS, QUID TE TIBI REDDAT
                    AMICUM.
                                        HOR.

SECTION I.

ON THE

BEAUTIES OF NATURE.

THAT senfibility to beauty, which,
when cultivated and improved,
we term Tafte, is univerfally diffufed
through the human fpecies: And it is
moft uniform with refpect to thofe objects, which, being out of our power,
are not liable to variation, from accident,
caprice, or fafhion. The verdant lawn,
the fhady grove, the variegated land-
fcape, the boundlefs ocean, and the
ftarry firmament, are contemplated with
pleafure by every attentive beholder.
But

But the emotions of different fpectators, though fimilar in kind, differ widely in degree: And to relifh, with full delight, the enchanting fcenes of nature, the mind muft be uncorrupted by avarice, fenfuality, or ambition; quick in her fenfibilities; elevated in her fentiments; and devout in her affections. He, who poffeffes fuch exalted powers of perception and enjoyment, may almoft fay, with the Poet,

" I care not, Fortune! what you me deny;
" You cannot rob me of free Nature's grace;
" You cannot fhut the windows of the fky,
" Thro' which Aurora fhews her brightening face;
" You cannot bar my conftant feet to trace
" The woods and lawns, by living ftream, at eve:
" Let health my nerves and finer fibres brace,
" And I their toys to the great children leave:
" Of fancy, reafon, virtue, nought can me bereave."*

Perhaps fuch ardent enthufiafm may not be compatible with the neceffary

* Thomfon's Caftle of Indolence.

toils,

toils, and active offices, which Providence has assigned to the generality of men. But there are none, to whom some portion of it may not prove advantageous; and if it were cherished, by each individual, in that degree which is consistent with the indispensable duties of his station, the felicity of human life would be considerably augmented. From this source, the refined and vivid, pleasures of the imagination are almost entirely derived: And the elegant arts owe their choicest beauties to a taste for the contemplation of nature. Painting and sculpture are express imitations of visible objects: And where would be the charms of poetry, if divested of the imagery and embellishments, which she borrows from rural scenes? Painters, statuaries, and poets, therefore, are always ambitious to acknowledge themselves the pupils of nature; and as their skill increases, they grow more and more delighted with every view of the animal

and

and vegetable world. But the pleafure refulting from admiration is tranfient; and to cultivate tafte, without regard to its influence on the paffions and affec-tions, " is to rear a tree for its bloffoms, " which is capable of yielding the richeft, " and moft valuable fruit."* Phyfical and moral beauty bear fo intimate a rela-tion to each other, that they may be confidered as different gradations in the fcale of excellence; and the knowledge and relifh of the former, fhould be deemed only a ftep to the nobler and more permanent enjoyments of the latter.

Whoever has vifited the Leafowes, in Shropfhire, muft have felt the force and propriety of an infcription, which meets the eye, at the entrance into thofe delightful grounds.

" Would you then tafte the tranquil fcene ?
" Be fure your bofoms be ferene ;

* Shenftone.

" Devoid

" Devoid of hate, devoid of ftrife,
" Devoid of all that poifons life :
" And much it 'vails you, in their place
" To graft the love of human race." *

Now fuch fcenes contribute powerfully to infpire that ferenity, which is
neceffary to enjoy, and to heighten their
beauties. By a fecret contagion, the
foul catches the harmony, which fhe
contemplates ; and the frame within, af-
fimilates itfelf to that which is without.
For,

" Who can forbear to fmile with Nature ? Can
" The ftormy paffions in the bofom roll,
" While every gale is peace, and every grove
" Is melody ?" †

* Shenftone.

† Thomfon's Seafons, firft Edit.

Horace, when he breaks forth into the animated exclamation,
　　" O, rus! quando ego te afpiciam, quandoque licebit
　　" Nunc veterum libris, nunc fomno et inertibus horis
　　" Ducere folicitæ jucunda oblivia vitæ ;"
feems to regret the want of that heartfelt complacency, which
the buftle, pomp, and pleafures of imperial Rome could not
afford.

In

In this state of sweet compofure, we become fufceptible of virtuous impreffions, from almoft every furrounding object. The patient ox is viewed with generous complacency; the guilelefs sheep, with pity; and the playful lamb raifes emotions of tendernefs and love. We rejoice with the horfe, in his liberty and exemption from toil, whilft he ranges at large through enamelled paftures; and the frolics of the colt would afford unmixed delight, did we not recollect the bondage, which he is foon to undergo. We are charmed with the fongs of birds, foothed with the buzz of infects, and pleafed with the fportive motions of fifhes, becaufe thefe are expreffions of enjoyment; and we exult in the felicity of the whole animated creation. Thus an equal and extenfive benevolence is called forth into exertion; and having *felt* a common intereft in the gratifications of inferior beings, we fhall be no longer

indifferent

indifferent to their fufferings, or become wantonly inftrumental in producing them.

It feems to be the intention of Providence, that the lower orders of animals fhould be fubfervient to the comfort, convenience, and fuftenance of man. But his right of dominion extends no farther; and if this right be exercifed with mildnefs, humanity, and juftice, the fubjects of his power will be no lefs benefitted, than himfelf. For various fpecies of living creatures are annually multiplied by human art, improved in their perceptive powers by human culture, and plentifully fed by human induftry. The relation, therefore, is reciprocal, between fuch animals and man; and he may fupply his own wants by the ufe of their labour, the produce of their bodies, and even the facrifice of their lives; whilft he co-operates with all-gracious Heaven, in promoting HAPPINESS, the great end of exiftence.

But

But though it be true, that *partial evil,* with refpect to different orders of fenfitive beings, may be *univerfal good*; and that it is a wife and benevolent inftitution of nature, to make deftruction itfelf, within certain limitations, the caufe of an increafe of life and enjoyment; yet a generous perfon will extend his compaffionate regards to every individual, that fuffers for his fake : And, whilft he fighs

> " Ev'n for the kid, or lamb, that pours its life
> " Beneath the bloody knife;"*

he will naturally be folicitous to mitigate pain, both in duration and degree, by the gentleft modes of inflicting it.

I am inclined to believe, however, that this fenfe of humanity would foon be obliterated, and that the heart would grow callous to every foft impreffion, were it not for the benignant influence

* Lord Lyttelton.

of

of the smiling face of nature. The Count de Lauzun, when imprisoned by Louis XIV. in the castle of Pignerol, amused himself, during a long period of time, with catching flies, and delivering them to be devoured by a rapacious spider. Such an entertainment was equally singular and cruel; and inconsistent, I believe, with his former character, and subsequent turn of mind. But his cell had no window; and received only a glimmering light, from an aperture in the roof. In less unfavourable circumstances, may we not presume, that instead of sporting with misery, he would have released the agonising flies; and bid them enjoy that freedom, of which he himself was bereaved?

But the taste for natural beauty is subservient to higher purposes, than those which have been enumerated: And the cultivation of it not only refines and humanises, but dignifies and exalts the

P   affections.

affections. It elevates them to the admiration and love of that Being, who is the Author of all that is fair, sublime, and good in the creation. Scepticism and irreligion are hardly compatible with the sensibility of heart,* which arises from a just and lively relish of the wisdom, harmony, and order subsisting in the world around us: And emotions of piety must spring up spontaneously in the bosom, that is in unison with all animated nature. Actuated by this divine inspiration, man finds a fane in every grove: And glowing with devout fervour, he joins his song to the universal chorus; or muses the praise of the Almighty, in more expressive silence. Thus they

  " Whom Nature's works can charm, with God himself·
  " Hold converse; grow familiar, day by day,
  " With his conceptions; act upon his plan;
  " And form to his, the relish of their souls."†

* See Gregory's Comparative View.   † Akenside.

SECTION

SECTION II.

ON

A GENERAL TASTE FOR THE

FINE ARTS.

THE analogy of physical to moral beauty, and the connection subsisting between a good heart, and a just relish for the general works of nature, have, I trust, been fully established. But, though all mankind are endued with the principle or faculty of taste, it often lies almost entirely dormant, for want of cultivation. The savage Indian, wholly

P 2

occupied

occupied in providing for the neceffities of life, traverfes the defart, and the flowery lawn, with equal indifference. Eager in the chafe, he fcarcely turns his eye, as he paffes along, to contemplate the golden beams of the fetting fun, reflected from the lake of Erie. Or if he quit his native wilds, in the fummer feafon, to fifh in the river Ohio, he fits in his canoe, inattentive to the awful cataract, and views the moft fplendid fcene in the creation, with flight and tranfient emotions. Nor are the generality of men, even in civilifed fociety, or in the higher walks of life, fully qualified to comprehend or to admire the *affemblage* of beauties, which the vifible creation prefents to the view of an enlightened imagination. Single objects, or detached parts, attract the notice and engrofs the attention: And the mind, by an eafy tranfition, paffes to the recognition and relifh of thofe operations

of

of human ſkill, which are their ſymbols, or repreſentations. For the elegant arts are all imitative in their eſſence and origin. Thus muſic, by the variation of its movements and tones, calls up, into the mind, ideas both of the natural, animal, and rational world. The murmuring brook, and boiſterous ocean; the ſtormy wind, and gentle zephyr; the wild roar of the lion, the bleating of the lamb, and the plaintive melody of the nightingale, are all within the compaſs of its mimetic enchantments. Theſe are extended even to the paſſions and emotions of the human heart; ſo as to typify anger, pity, remorſe, delight, and ſorrow. Painting occupies a ſtill wider field of ſimilitude and aſſociation; diſplaying all thoſe objects, which are known to us, in nature, by diverſity of figure, or the various ſhades of colour. Even motions and ſounds may be expreſſed by this wonderful art. For, as

P 3

they

they are accompanied, in many inftances, with a certain configuration, or pofition of parts, the fign is readily adopted for the thing fignified. And we fee or hear upon the canvas, the horfe *ftarting* aghaft at the fudden view of the lion; the foldier *running* towards his dying general with the news of victory; the cock *crowing* at the denial of Peter; and the water-fall *dafhing* againft the rocks below.*

Poetry, under which term I mean to comprehend all numerous and rhetorical compofition, derives moft of its charms from allufions, fimilies, metaphors, or defcriptions; and thefe are obvioufly imitative. In this way, its powers are fo tranfcendant, that even a fingle epithet will fometimes produce a reprefentation more picturefque, than the pencil of Pouffin, or Salvator Rofa, ever ex-

* Mr. Stubbs's Picture. The death of General Wolfe, &c.

hibited.

hibited.   The firſt line, in the following ſtanza of Gray's elegy, will afford an example, and a proof, of what is here advanced.

Now fades the *glimmering* landſcape on the ſight,
And all the air a ſolemn ſtillneſs holds,
Save where the beetle wheels his droning flight,
And drowſy tinklings lull the diſtant folds. *

The accuracy and force of the word *glimmering* muſt be felt by any one, who has viewed, with attention, an extenſive proſpect, about an hour after ſun-ſet.

The mimetic arts have ſome advantages over nature herſelf; for the imitations, with which they preſent us, are generally agreeable, even though their archetypes be, in themſelves, indifferent or diſguſting. The mind delights in compariſon; and this pleaſure is heightened

* Gray's Elegy.

P 4   by

by the recognition of refemblance, and by the contemplation of ingenious defign, or mafterly execution. Who can read Mr. Gay's defcription of a poor, benighted traveller, without being charmed at the verifimilitude of the narration; which is, at once, fo clear, fo difcriminative, and circumftantial, that we become, as it were, fpectators of a fcene, which either in its parts, or in the whole, is exactly correfpondent to our recollection and experience.

It is evident, therefore, that the fine arts have, for their object, the gratification of the fame faculty, which perceives and relifhes the charms of nature. And by analogy we may infer, that the exercife, which they give to the tafte, is favourable to the virtuous affections of the heart. This truth has been fo long acknowledged, that the obfervation of

* Ovid.

the

the Poet is now received, as an eftablifhed maxim in ethics ;

Ingenuas didiciffe fideliter artes
Emollit mores, nec finit effe feros. **

But the validity of this canon is not to be admitted, without fome reftriction. The energies of mufic, painting, and poetry, are fo powerful and multifarious, that they have, at command, all the emotions and paffions of the foul.

- - - - - - - - - - - - pectus inaniter angunt,
Irritant, mulcent, falfis terroribus implent. *

They may excite or reftrain, kindle or extinguifh paffion, and thus, according to their application, become the inftruments either of vice, or of virtue. They are incident, likewife, to numberlefs adventitious affociations, which, counteracting or diverfifying their natural and original tendency, may make them adminifter to vanity, oftentation, pride,

* Hor. Epift. I. Lib. 2.

envy,

envy, and jealousy. Such dispositions are sometimes found in the professors of these arts; and the display of them, in men of distinguished genius and merit, raises in our minds a painful struggle of discordant emotions.*

Whoever, therefore, yields himself, implicitly, to the magic delusions of the fine arts, is in danger of having his judgment impaired, his heart corrupted, and his capacity destroyed for the ordinary duties and enjoyments of life. To this source may be traced all the follies and extravagance of what is termed VERTU. Admiration stimulates the desire of possession, however immoderate the price; possession turns the admiration of the object to ourselves; and this is suc-

---

* Who would not laugh, if such a one there be?
Who would not weep, if Atticus were he?   POPE.

No reflection is meant, by the quotation of these lines, on the very respectable character to whom they allude. They were dictated by resentment, and reprobated by some of the Poet's best friends.

ceeded

ceeded by a fond and abſurd impatience to diſplay a ſuperiority over others, both in taſte and property.

> What brought Sir Viſto's ill got wealth to waſte?
> Some dæmon whiſper'd, " Viſto, have a taſte."
> Heaven viſits with a taſte the wealthy fool;
> And needs no rod, but Ripley with a rule. *

But it is further to be obſerved, that, as an acute reliſh for beauty, and a quick diſcernment of deformity are, in a certain proportion, neceſſarily connected together; the latter may become predominant, through pride, affectation, or too frequent indulgence. Whenever this happens, taſte will prove the inſtrument of pain, and not of pleaſure: And the faſtidious feelings of diſguſt, ſo often excited, will be transferred, from the works of human ſkill, to human life; rendering the temper petulant, moroſe, and ſelfiſh. But a perverſion of the

* Pope's Moral Eſſays.

powers

powers of the imagination is no argument againſt their proper culture, and
well regulated application. For reaſon
itſelf is liable to abuſe; and philoſophy
and religion have been rendered ſub-
ſervient to ſcepticiſm and ſuperſtition.

MISCELLANEOUS

OBSERVATIONS

ON THE ALLIANCE OF

NATURAL HISTORY, AND PHILOSOPHY,

WITH POETRY.

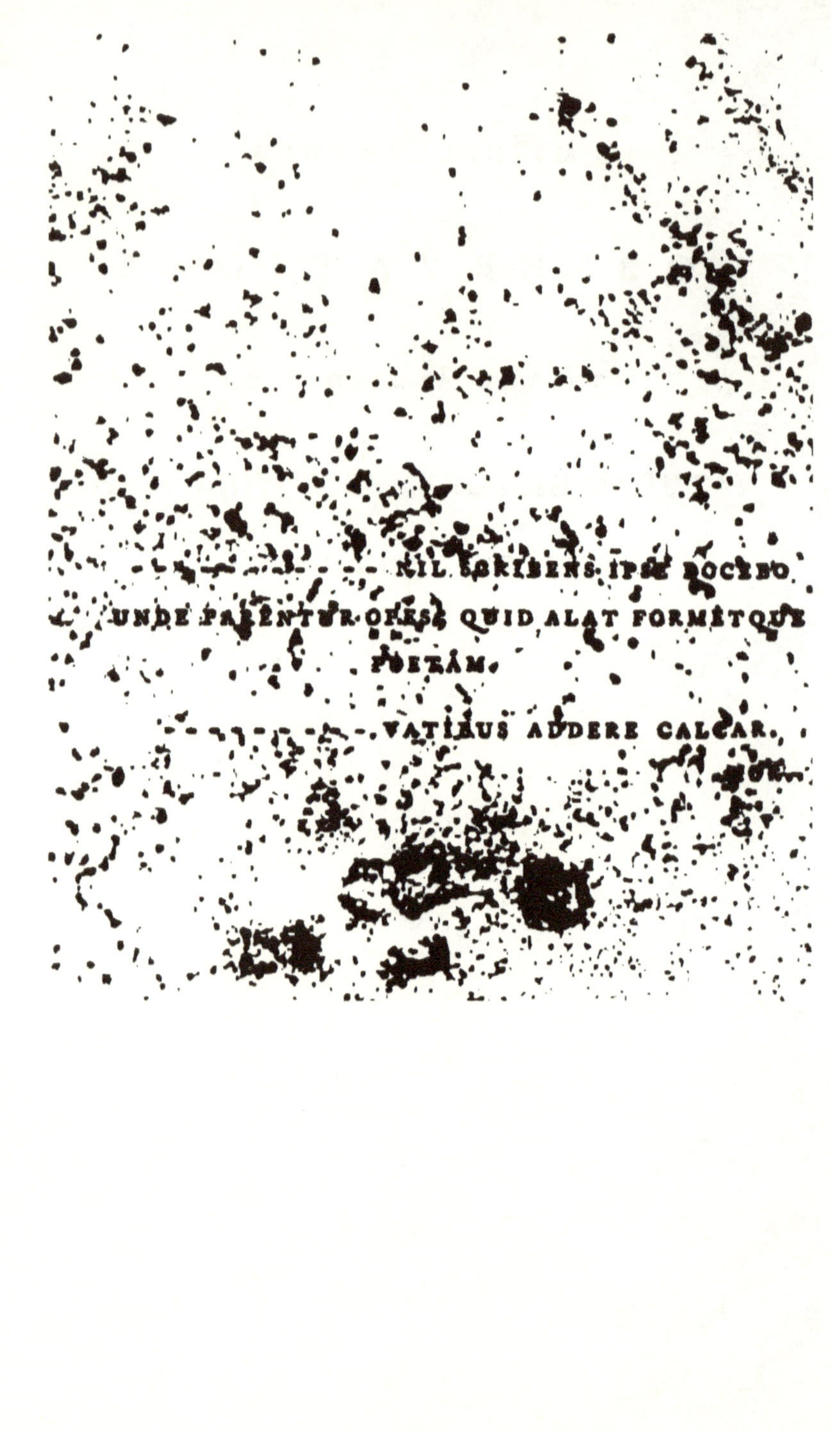

NIL SCRIBENS IPSE DOCEBO
UNDE PARENTUR OPES, QUID ALAT FORMETQUE
POETAM.

VATIBUS ADDERE CALCAR.

MISCELLANEOUS

OBSERVATIONS

ON THE ALLIANCE OF

NATURAL HISTORY, AND PHILOSOPHY,

WITH POETRY.*

THE maxim of lord Verulam, that "knowledge is power," is no lefs applicable to poefy, than to philofophy. For whether we engage in this delightful purfuit as an art, or as a fcience, it is evident that the ability to convey, and the capacity to relifh its peculiar plea-

* In this Effay, the author has confined his views, chiefly, to the application of natural knowledge, to that branch of the poetic art, which relates to DESCRIPTION; referving, for fome future occafion, the alliance of phyfics, with poetical IMAGERY and MORAL ANALOGY.

fures,

fures, muſt be exactly proportioned to our acquaintance with the means either of communicating or enjoying them. The works of creation are the great ſtorehouſe, where theſe means are to be ſought. And an inquiſitive attention to every ſurrounding object is eſſential to the poet, and highly uſeful to the lover of poetry. He, who extends his re-ſearches beyond the ſurface of things, will find that the treaſures of nature are inexhauſtible. For it is literally, no leſs than metaphorically true, that

> - - - - Many a gem, of pureſt ray ſerene,
> The dark unfathom'd caves of ocean bear,
> Full many a flower is born to bluſh unſeen,
> And waſte its ſweetneſs on the deſart air. *

Yet few have been the labourers in this rich harveſt of ſcience, ſince the days of Theocritus; and the paſtoral deſcrip-tions and images of that ancient Sicilian bard, have been uſed like hereditary

* Gray's Elegy.

property,

property, by all fucceeding poets. In the ruder ages of the world, the modes of life were peculiarly favourable to the obfervation of nature. Rural fcenery was continually before the eyes; and the culture of land, or the care of fheep and cattle, conftituted the occupation of the greateft perfonages. This furnifhed a rich fupply of original materials, which muft for ever be withheld from thofe, who immure themfelves in cities, and contemplate only the operations of art. Writers, therefore, of this clafs, are humbly fatisfied to be mere copyifts of others; and adopt, without referve, the figures, allufions, and reprefentations of their poetical predeceffors. But fcience, which is borrowed, is often mifunderftood: And it is not in the power, even of genius itfelf, to obviate the miftakes which are committed through ignorance. Who, for inftance, can notice the countenance of the Ox, without perceiving, that it difplays meeknefs, patience, and the

Q

moft

moſt inoffenſive diſpoſition;* and that the eyes of this animal are of no unuſual dimenſion? Yet, in many verſions of Homer, that divine poet, ſo converſant with zoology, is made to ſtile the artful, proud, and paſſionate queen of the gods "Ox-eyed Juno." This miſtake of the tranſlators has evidently ariſen, from the want of attention to nature. And M. Dacier has ſhewn, that the particle Cʊ is only an augmentative, ſignifying (*valde*) large-eyed; and that it has no direct relation to the ox. The error, which Dr. Young has fallen into, in his paraphraſe on Job, is more pardonable; becauſe an Engliſh poet, who has never ſeen the Crocodile, might be ignorant that his eyes are remarkably ſmall. This animal is ſuppoſed to be the Leviathan, deſcribed in the 41ſt chapter of that book. And, if the explanation be true,

---

* Thomſon thus deſcribes the ox:

     - - - - - - - - - And the plain ox,
That honeſt, harmleſs, guileleſs animal.

the

the following paſſage muſt have a reference to the brightneſs, and not to the
magnitude, of his organs of ſight, as
my friend Mr. Aikin has judiciouſly remarked.* *By his neezings a light doth
ſhine; and his eyes are like the eyelids of the
morning.* Dr. Young, by a miſconcep-
tion of the original, has rendered this
ſtrong figure ſtill more hyperbolical.

" Large is his front; and when his burniſh'd eyes
" Lift their *broad* lids, the morning ſeems to riſe."

In a former eſſay I have remarked,
concerning the mimetic powers of poetry,
that a ſingle word will ſometimes produce a repreſentation more pictureſque,
than the pencil of Pouſſin, or of Salvator
Roſa, ever exhibited. And the obſervation was exemplified by this line of
Mr. Gray;

" Now fades the glimmering landſcape on the
ſight, "

* See his elegant and ingenious Eſſay, on the Application
of Natural Hiſtory to Poetry.

in

in which the accuracy and force of the epithet *glimmering* will be felt by any one, who has viewed, with attention, an extensive prospect, about an hour after sun-set.* But a gentleman of this county, who has inserted the foregoing line in a very elegant little poem, by an unfortunate transposition, has entirely destroyed its beauty, truth, and energy.

"Now fades the landscape on the *glimmering sight*."

Many original writers, of the most distinguished reputation, have deviated widely from nature, by adopting facts and opinions without examination, or on insufficient authority. Thus the poet Lucretius, who flourished about fifty years before the Christian æra, has sanctioned the vulgar error, that, in the JAUNDICE, objects are painted on the retina, of the same colour with that, which tinges the external coat of the

* Essay on the Advantages of a Taste for Nature and the Fine Arts.

eye;

eye; and has given a theory of it in conformity to the philosophy of the Epicurean school.

> *Lurida præterea fiunt quæcunque tuentur*
> *Arquati, quia luroris de corpore eorum*
> *Semina multa fluunt, simulacris obvia rerum;*
> *Multaque sunt oculis in eorum denique mista,*
> *Quæ contage sua palloribus omnia pingunt.* *

Besides, whatever jaundic'd eyes do view,
Look pale, as well as those, and yellow too,
For lurid parts fly off, with nimble wings,
And meet the distant coming forms of things:
And others lurk within the eyes, and seize,
And stain, with pale, the entering images. †

Mr. Pope has authorised the same observation, in his Essay on Criticism.

" All seems infected, that th' infected spy,
" As all looks yellow to the jaundic'd eye."

And the like mistaken allusion is more than once repeated in an admirable poem, lately published by Mr. Hayley.

* Lucretius, Lib. IV. line 333.
† Creech's Transf. of Lucret. Book IV. line 344.

" The

" The bards of Britain, with unjaundic'd eyes,
" Will glory to behold fuch rivals rife. *

" On faireft names, from every blemifh free ;
" Save what the jaundic'd eyes of party fee. "

I am inclined to believe there is no fufficient foundation for this opinion. Galen indeed fpeaks of yellow vifion, as common to icteric patients ; and Sextus Empyricus has delivered the fame account : But their relation is neither confirmed by experience, nor confonant to reafon. In the worft cafes of the jaundice, now known, this fymptom has no exiftence ; and I do not find it noticed in the records of Aretæus, Celfus, or Hippocrates.

The fuppofition, that the fertilifing quality of snow arifes from nitrous falts, which it is fuppofed to acquire in the act of freezing, is void of foundation ;

* On Epic Poetry, Epift. IV.

becaufe

becaufe the moft accurate experiments have demonftrated, that it contains no nitre, and only a fmall portion of calcareous earth. Falfe philofophy, fays an eminent chemift,* firft gave rife to this idea, and poetry has contributed to diffufe the error. Thus Mr. Philips;

---------- O may'ft thou often fee
Thy furrows whiten'd 'by the woolly rain,
Nutritious; fecret nitre lurks within
The porous wet; quickening the languid glebe.

But the following lines, of Mr. Thomfon, do not appear to me to be liable to the fame objection. For the term *falts*, with the annexed epithet *little*, may be applied, without much poetical licence, to the cryftals of water, formed by freezing.

What art thou, froft?
Is not thy potent energy unfeen,
Myriads of *little falts*, or hook'd, or fhap'd
Like double wedges, and diffus'd immenfe
Thro' water, earth and ether?

* Dr. Watfon, now Bifhop of Landaff, in his Chemical Effays.

The

The operation of froſt is here aſcribed to its mechanical powers. ·For, by binding the ſurface of the earth, it arreſts the exhalations, as they aſcend from the parts below; and thus retains a nutritious *pabulum*, to be applied, at the proper ſeaſon, to the roots of plants. But it chiefly meliorates the ſoil, by pulveriſing the particles which compoſe it, and fitting them for the abſorption of the vernal dews and rains.

Whenever PHILOSOPHY is introduced into poetry, truth, for the moſt part, is eſſential to its power of giving pleaſure. And our great epic writer ſeems to deſcend, ſometimes, from the majeſty of his work, by mixing, with modern diſcoveries, the groundleſs opinions of the ancients. Thus, when Raphael addreſſes Adam, concerning the great ſyſtem of nature, he ſays,

-------------- Other ſuns, perhaps,
With their attendant moons, thou wilt deſcry,
Communicating *male* and *female* light. *

* Milton's Paradiſe Loſt, Book VIII. line 148.

The

·The idea of *male* light being communicated by the *sun*, and *female* light by the *moon*, probably originated, in the mind of Milton, from his intimate acquaintance with the writings of Pliny; who mentions, as a tradition, "that " the fun is a mafculine ftar, drying all " things, but that the moon is a foft and " feminine ftar, of diffolving power: " And that thus the balance of nature " is preferved; fome of the ftars binding " the elements; and others loofening " them." *

The HARMONY of the SPHERES, or mufical revolution of the heavenly bodies in their feveral orbits, was firft taught by the Pythagoreans; who feem to have

* *Solis ardore ficcatur liquor; et hoc effe mafculum fidus accepimus, torrens cuncta forbenfque.---E contrario ferunt lunam femineum ac molle fidus, atque nocturnum folvere humorem.---Ita penfari naturæ vices, femperque fufficere, aliis fiderum elementa cogentibus, aliis vero fundentibus.* Hift. Nat. Lib. II. Cap. 100. See alfo the notes to Newton's Edit. of Par. Loft.

derived

derived this fanciful doctrine from analogy. For it was obferved, by thefe philofophers, that a mufical chord produces the fame note, as one double in length, when the force is quadruple with which the latter is ftretched : Hence they fuppofed that the gravity of a planet is quadruple the gravity of a planet, at a double diftance. And as any mufical chord may become unifon to a leffer chord, of the fame kind, if its tenfion be increafed in the fame proportion as the fquare of its length is greater; fo the gravity of a planet may become equal to the gravity of another planet, nearer to the fun, provided it be increafed in proportion as the fquare of its diftance from the fun is greater. If, therefore, mufical chords be extended from the fun to each planet, to bring them into unifon, it would be requifite, to increafe or diminifh their tenfions, in the fame proportions, as would be fufficient to render

the

the gravity of the planets equal.* This notion of the Pythagoreans is fo pleafing to the imagination, that it is not furprifing the poets have adopted it. And Milton has given fuch a view of it, as wants nothing but philofophical truth to render it delightful.

> Myftical dance, which yonder ftarry fphere
> Of planets, and of fix'd, in all her wheels
> Refembles neareft; mazes intricate,
> Eccentric, intervolv'd, yet regular,
> Then moft, when moft irregular they feem;
> And in their motions harmony divine
> So fmooths her charming tones, that God's
>   own ear
> Liftens delighted. †

Mr. Pope has not only fuppofed the actual exiftence of this heavenly harmony, but that it is poffible the human ear might have been fo conftituted, as to have been fenfible of it.

* Vid. Plin. Lib. II. Cap. 22. Macrob. Lib. II. Cap. 1. See alfo, Maclaurin's account of Sir Ifaac Newton's Philofophical Difcoveries, page 34.

† Paradife Loft, Book V. line 620.

If Nature thunder'd in his opening ears,
And ſtunn'd him with the muſic of the ſpheres;
How would he wiſh that heav'n had left him ſtill,
The whiſp'ring zephyr, and the purling rill?*

Thoſe, who are in poſſeſſion of the firſt or ſecond edition of Thomſon's Seaſons, will find a groſs geographical miſtake, in the hymn which is annexed to them. Towards the cloſe of this beautiful poem, the author expreſſes his pious confidence in the univerſal wiſdom, and impartial benevolence of the Deity; and aſſerts, that the ſame regular ſeaſons, which he had deſcribed with ſuch fervour of delight in the preceding work, are equally experienced in every part of the globe.

------- God is ever preſent, ever felt,
In the void waſte, as in the city full;
Roll the *ſame kindred ſeaſons* round the world,
In all *apparent,* wiſe and good in all.

* Eſſay on Man, Ep. I. ver. 201.

The

The two laſt lines are omitted, in the ſubſequent editions of this poem.

The SYSTEM of PHILOSOPHY, which is now received, independent of its ſuperiority in point of truth, infinitely exceeds in extent, elevation, and grandeur, that of the ancients. The poet, therefore, ſhould be well verſed in the ſcience of phyſics, not only becauſe he can ſeldom deviate from it,* without injury to his

---

* In the following lines, the thought becomes low, by being unphiloſophical.

     - - - - - - - - - - - - - O thieviſh night,
Why ſhould'ſt thou, but for ſome felonious end,
In thy *dark lantborn* thus cloſe up the ſtars
That Nature hung in heaven, and filled their *lamps*
With everlaſting *oil.*
                    Milton's Comus.

The ſentiment is more brilliant, in a ſubſequent paſſage of this poem, but not more ſolid. And it is rendered abſurd by the leaſt reflection, on the impoſſibility of ſinking the vaſt orbs of the ſun and moon, in the ocean; or, as it is here improperly ſtiled, the *flat ſea.*

    Virtue could ſee to do what virtue would,
    By her own radiant light; though ſun and moon
    Wete in the *flat ſea* ſunk.
              Id.

com-

compofitions, but becaufe thefe may de-
rive from it fublimity, embellifhment,
or grace. Aftronomy, in particular, furnifhes fuch magnificent ideas, and boundlefs views, that imagination can hardly
grafp, much lefs exalt or amplify them.
" The objects which we commonly call
" great," fays an eminent writer, " vanifh,
" when we contemplate the vaft body of
" the earth ; the terraqueous globe itfelf
" is foon loft in the folar fyftem. In
" fome parts it is feen as a diftant ftar ;
" in others it is unknown ; or vifible
" only at rare times, to vigilant obfervers.
" The fun itfelf dwindles into a ftar ;
" Saturn's vaft orbit, and the orbits of
" all the comets, crowd into a point,
" when viewed from numberlefs fpaces
" between the earth and the neareft of
" the fixed ftars. Other funs kindle light
" to illuminate other fyftems, where our
" fun's rays are unperceived ; but they
" alfo are fwallowed up in the vaft ex-
" panfe. Even all the fyftems of the
" ftars,

" ftars, that fparkle in the cleareft fky,
" muft poffefs a corner only of that fpace,
" through which fuch fyftems are dif-
" perfed : Since more ftars are difcovered
" in one conftellation, by the telefcope,
" than the naked eye perceives in the
" whole heavens. After we have rifen
" fo high, and left all definite meafures
" far behind us, we find ourfelves no
" nearer to a term or limit; for all this
" is nothing to what may be difplayed
" in the infinite expanfe, beyond the re-
" moteft ftars that have hitherto been dif-
" covered."*   This defcription, though
delivered in the chafte language of a
mathematician, is, in fentiment, fo truly
fublime, that it wants nothing but numbers to conftitute it poetry. And, in the
following lines, it appears with all the
charms of grace and harmony.

- - - - - - - - - - - - - - Seiz'd in thought,
On Fancy's wild and roving wing I fail
From the green borders of the peopled earth,

* Maclaurin's View of Sir Ifaac Newton's Difcoveries, p. 16.

And

And the pale moon, her duteous, fair attendant;
From folitary Mars; from the vaft orb
Of Jupiter, whofe huge gigantic bulk
Dances in ether, like the lighteft leaf;
To the dim verge, the fuburbs of the fyftem,
Where cheerlefs Saturn 'midft his wat'ry moons
Girt with a lucid zone, majeftic fits
In gloomy grandeur, like an exil'd queen
Amongft her weeping handmaids: fearlefs thence
I launch into the tracklefs deeps of fpace,
Where burning round ten thoufand funs appear,
Of elder beam; which afk no leave to fhine
Of our terreftrial ftar, nor borrow light
From the proud regent of our fcanty day;
Sons of the morning, firft-born of creation,
And only lefs than Him who marks their track,
And guides their fiery wheels.   Here muft I ftop?
Or is there aught beyond? What hand, unfeen,
Impels me onward, through the glowing orbs
Of habitable nature; far remote,
To the dread confines of eternal night,
To folitudes of vaft unpeopled fpace,
The defarts of creation, wide and wild;
Where embryo fyftems, and unkindled funs
Sleep in the womb of chaos! Fancy droops,
And thought, aftonifh'd, ftops her bold career! *

* Mrs. Barbauld's Evening Meditation.

Homer,

Homer, whofe knowledge of the magnitude and diftances of the heavenly bodies, muft have been very confined, never difplays a more glowing imagination, than when he introduces them to our notice. And no one can view his animated picture of a moonlight and ftarry night, without feeling himfelf tranfported to the fcene, which it exhibits.

As when the moon, refulgent lamp of night,
O'er heaven's clear azure fpreads her facred
    light;
When not a breath difturbs the deep ferene,
And not a cloud o'ercafts the folemn fcene;
Around her throne the vivid planets roll,
And ftars unnumber'd gild the glowing pole;
O'er the dark trees a yellower verdure fhed,
And tip with filver every mountain's head;
Then fhine the vales, the rocks in profpect rife,
A flood of glory burfts from all the fkies;
The confcious fwains, rejoicing in the fight,
Eye the blue vault, and blefs the ufeful light. *

* Pope's Homer's Iliad, Book VIII. line 687.

R   Mr.

Mr. Pope has tranflated this paffage with fingular felicity; and perhaps it may be the faftidioufnefs of criticifm to remark, that a *refulgent moon* is not compatible with *vivid* planets, and *glowing ftars*; becaufe thefe fainter lights are eclipfed by the fplendour of that luminary. But, though Homer, probably, did not mean to introduce a full moon, as his commentator Euftathius has obferved, yet a judicious Poet has chofen to leave this bright orb out of the evening fcenery, which fhe has fo admirably pourtrayed.

- - - - - - - - - - - - - - Nature's felf is hufh'd;
And but a fcattered leaf, which ruftles thro'
The thick-wove foliage; not a found is heard
To break the midnight air.
- - - - - - - - - - - - - - 'Tis now the hour
When Contemplation, from her funlefs haunts,
Moves forward; and with radiant finger points
Where, one by one, the living eyes of heaven
Awake, quick kindling o'er the face of ether
One boundlefs blaze; ten thoufand trembling fires
And dancing luftres, where th' unfteady eye,

Reftlefs

Reftlefs and dazzled, wanders unconfin'd
O'er all this field of glories. *

It may be amufing to contraft the foregoing defcriptions of the night, with thofe recorded by Mr. Macpherfon, in his tranflation of the poems of Offian. Five bards, paffing the night in the houfe of a Caledonian chief, went out feverally to make their obfervations; and returned with an extempore defcription of the night, which, as appears from the poem, was in the month of October. I fhall here recite part of the compofition of the fourth bard, as it is moft analogous to the paffages, above quoted.

" Night is calm and fair; blue, ftarry,
" fettled is night. The winds, with the
" clouds, are gone. They fink behind
" the hill. The moon is upon the moun-
" tain. Trees glifter; ftreams fhine on
" the rock. Bright rolls the fettled lake;
" bright the ftream of the vale.

* Mrs. Barbauld's Even. Med.

" The

" The breezes drive the blue mist,
" flowly over the narrow vale. It rifes
" on the hill, and joins its head to hea-
" ven.—Night is fettled, calm, blue,
" ftarry, bright with the moon. Re-
" ceive me not, my friends; for lovely is
" the night."*

In fouthern latitudes the HEAVENLY
BODIES are far more refplendent, than
when viewed through the thick atmofphere of Britain. It is faid, that, in
Jamaica, the *milky way* is tranfcendently
bright, and that the planet Venus appears like a little moon, glittering with
fo vivid a beam, as to render vifible the
fhadows of trees, buildings, and other
objects.† The fetting fun, in that ifland,
exhibits a fpectacle peculiarly auguft.
His circumference being enlarged by
the interpofing vapours, and the refrac-

* Offian's Croma, p. 255, 4to Edition.

† Hift. of Jamaica, Book II. p. 371.

tion

tion of the rays of light retaining in view his glorious orb, he feems to reſt awhile, from his career, on the fummit of the mountains. Then he fuddenly vaniſhes, leaving a train of fplendour, which ſtreaks the clouds with the moſt lively and variegated tints, that the happieſt fancy can conceive.* In defcribing fuch a fpectacle as this, the majeſty of the great luminary generally abforbs the whole attention of the poet; and he takes little notice of the effect of the fun's declination, on terreſtrial objects. Yet it is certain, that a landſcape, of fmall extent, never appears more beautiful, than at the clofe of a fummer's day. Several caufes then confpire to give a richnefs to the fcene, and no one fo powerfully, as the heightened verdure of the herbage, arifing, probably, from the combination of blue and yellow colours, reflected, at the fame time, from the golden clouds, and azure ſky. Perhaps

* Hiſt. of Jamaica, Book II. p. 372.

R 3   the

the increafed refraction, and foftened luftre of the evening rays of light, may alfo contribute to this effect. For the herbage at that time appears, not only more green, but more copious too: Infomuch that a pafture, which looks *bare* at noon, feems to abound in grafs at fun-fet. When thick black vapours hover about the weftern fun, and prefent only fmall illumined edges, I have obferved a circle of green, furrounding his difc; an appearance, which I know not how to account for, but from the union, above defcribed, of blue and yellow rays. This phenomenon I faw, in great perfection, as I was lately travelling over the mountains, which divide the counties of Lancafter and York. The day was wet and ftormy; and the war of elements, which I beheld, gave me fome faint idea of what is experienced on the Alps and Andes; where the traveller views clouds at his feet, and corufcations of lightening darting, on all fides, below him.

him. Numberless meteors, which are unknown on the plain, present themselves to his astonished sight; such as circular rainbows, parhelia, the shadow of the mountain projected on the air, and his own image adorned with a kind of glory, round the head.* How tremendous is the account, which Don Ulloa has given, of his station on the top of Cotopaxi, a mountain in Peru, more than three geographical miles above the level of the sea! Here he was stationed, a considerable length of time, for the purpose of measuring a degree of the meridian; and the hardships which he suffered, from the intenseness of the cold, and the storms to which he was exposed, almost exceed belief. "The sky," says he, "was generally obscured with thick fogs; "but, when these were dispersed, and "the clouds moved, by their gravity, "nearer the surface of the earth, they

* Ulloa, Vol. I. Acad. Par. 1744. Priestley on Light and Colours, page 599, &c.

R 4

"fur-

" furrounded the mountain to a vaſt dif-
" tance, repreſenting the ſea, with our
" rock, like an iſland in the center of
" it.　When this happened, we heard
" the horrid noiſes of the tempeſts,
" which difcharged themſelves on Quito,
" and the neighbouring countries.　We
" ſaw the lightenings iſſue from the
" clouds, and heard the thunders roll
" far beneath us.　And, whilſt the lower
" regions were involved in tempeſts of
" thunder and rain, we enjoyed a de-
" lightful ſerenity.　The wind was huſh-
" ed, the ſky clear, and the enlivening
" rays of the ſun moderated the ſeverity
" of the cold."*　How would a ſcene,
like this, have been felt and deſcribed
by the Poet, of whom it is ſaid,

- - - - - - - - - - - - - - - When lightening fires
The arch of heaven, and thunders rock the ground;
When furious whirlwinds rend the howling air,
And ocean, groaning from his loweſt bed,

* Ulloa's Voyage, Vol. I. p. 231.

Heaves

Heaves his tempeftuous billows to the fky:
Amid the mighty uproar, while below
The nations tremble, Shakefpear looks abroad
From fome high cliff, fuperior, and enjoys
The elemental war.*

The awful and gloomy grandeur of the mountainous fcenery of Peru is, perhaps, lefs favourable to the defcriptive powers of the poet, than the profpects which fome of the Alpine countries of Europe afford. In the cultivated diftricts of Switzerland, particularly, the views furnifh the happieft combination of the fublime and beautiful. And I fhall give a fhort abftract of the obfervations made, by a late traveller, on the Mole, a mountain, which rifes near five thoufand feet above the lake of Geneva, and is fituated about eighteen miles eaftward of that city. " In my afcent," fays Sir George Shuckburgh, " I faw the fun, rifing be-
" hind one of the neighbouring Alps,

* Akenfide's Pleafures of Imagination, Book III. line 590.

" with

" with a moſt beautiful effect; and the
" ſhadow of the mountain, we were then
" upon, extended fifteen or twenty miles
" weſt. Before me, at ſome diſtance,
" was ſpread the plain, in which lay
" Geneva and the lake; behind me roſe
" the Dole, and the long chain of Mont
" Jura. A little to the left, and much
" nearer, lay Mont Saleve, which, from
" this height, appeared an inconſiderable
" hill. To the right and left, nothing
" but immenſe rocks, and pointed moun-
" tains, of every poſſible ſhape, form-
" ing tremendous precipices. In the
" vale beneath, ſeveral little hamlets,
" and the moſt beautiful paſturages,
" with the river Arve, winding and
" ſoftening the ſcene. From whence
" aroſe a thick evaporation, collecting
" itſelf into clouds, which, on the lake,
" that was quite covered with them,
" had the appearance of a ſea of cotton;
" the ſun's beams playing on the upper
" ſurface of them, with thoſe tints, which
" are

" are feen in a fine evening. To the
" fouth weft, appeared the lake of An-
" necy; behind us lay the Glacieres,
" and, amongft them, towering above
" all the reft, ftood Mount Blanc. The
" circumference of the horizon might
" be about two hundred Englifh miles;
" and though not one of the moft exten-
" five, yet certainly one of the moft
" varied in the world."*

It is with a reluctance, fimilar, perhaps,
to what this philofophical traveller experienced, when he defcended from the
Mole, that I quit the imaginary vifion
of this enchanting fcene. But it is neceffary to remark, that, however ftriking
fuch complex and fublime reprefentations
may be, they can only be introduced
occafionally by the poet; whofe talents
for defcription fhould be chiefly exercifed
in the judicious felection and picturefque

* Philofoph. Tranfact. 1777, p. 536.

difplay

difplay of fmall groups, or individual objects. Like the magnet, he muft draw forth what is valuable, even from the rudeft materials; and nicely difcriminate, in every furrounding object, thofe attributes, which can be rendered fubfervient to his art. We are informed, that Thomfon was wont to wander whole days and nights in the country: And, in fuch fequeftered walks, he acquired, by the moft minute attention, a knowledge of all the myfteries of nature. Thefe he has wrought into his Seafons with the colouring of Titian, the wildnefs of Salvator Rofa, and the energy of Raphael.

Milton appears to have been no lefs familiar with nature, than Thomfon, and equally happy in his portraits of her moft pleafing forms. He catches every diftinguifhing feature; and gives to what he defcribes, fuch glowing tints of life and reality, that we have it, as it were,

in

in full view before our eyes. How perfect is the image, in the following lines !

- - - - - - - - - The fwan, with *arched neck*
Between her *white wings mantling, proudly rows*
Her ftate, with *oary feet*.[*]

Indeed the whole account of the creation, which the Archangel relates to Adam, is fo engaging and picturefque, that it would fully refute the criticifm of a learned Italian, if the poem contained no other beauties of a fimilar kind. "The poets beyond the Alps," fays Abbè Winckelmann, " fpeak *figuratively*, but " without *painting*. The ftrange and " fometimes terrifying figures, which " conftitute almoft all the grandeur of " Milton, are by no means the *objects* of " a *pencil*, but rather feem beyond the " reach of *painting*."[†] Surely the de-

[*] Paradife Loft, Book VII. line 438.
[†] Hiftoire des l'Arts chez les Anciens.

fcription

fcription of the fwan, above recited, might be copied on the canvas, by any artiſt, of tolerable genius. As Milton derived his knowledge of this beautiful bird from actual obſervation, he has not fallen into the error of the ancient poets, who have, almoſt univerſally, aſcribed to it a muſical voice. Callimachus terms it " Apollo's tuneful fongſter ; " and Horace compliments Pindar with the epithet " *Dircæan fwan.*"* Such improprieties clearly evince the importance of natural knowledge to the poet.

The polity of ʀooᴋs is almoſt con-ſtituted with as much order and wiſdom, as that of ants, bees, and beavers ; and their attachment to places contiguous

* *Multa Dircæum levat aura Cycnum*
    Tendit Antoni, quoties in altos
    Nubium tractus.   Ode II. Lib. 4.
In the addreſs to Melpomene, he ſays,
    O mutis quoque piſcibus
    Donatura Cycni, ſi libeat, ſonum.   Ode III.

to

to the dwellings of men, not only affords us frequent opportunities of obferving them, but interefts us, at the fame time, in their well-being and prefervation. Thefe birds, therefore, furnifh the poet with various topics, for the difplay of his art; and the following incident, by a little colouring, might be wrought into a pathetic picture. A large colony of rooks had fubfifted, many years, in a grove, on the banks of the river Irwell, near Manchefter. One ferene evening, I placed myfelf within the view of it, and marked, with attention, the various labours, paftimes, and evolutions of this crowded fociety. The idle members amufed themfelves with chacing each other, through endlefs mazes; and, in their flight, they made the air refound with an infinitude of difcordant noifes. In the midft of thefe playful exertions, it unfortunately happened, that one rook, by a fudden turn, ftruck his beak againft the wing of another. The fufferer inftantly

ftantly fell into the river. A general cry of diftrefs enfued. The birds hovered, with every expreffion of anxiety, over their diftreffed companion. Animated by their fympathy, and perhaps by the language of counfel, known to themfelves, he fprung into the air, and by one ftrong effort, reached the point of a rock, which projected into the water. The exultation became loud and univerfal; but, alas! it was foon changed into notes of lamentation. For the poor wounded bird, in attempting to fly towards his neft, dropt again into the river, and was drowned, amidft the moans of his whole fraternity.

The habitudes of the domeftic breed of POULTRY cannot, poffibly, efcape obfervation: And every one muft have noticed the fierce jealoufy of the cock,

Whofe breaft with ardour flames, as on he walks,
Graceful, and crows defiance. *

* Thomfon's Spring, line 772.

It

It fhould feem that this jealoufy is not confined to his rivals, but may fome-times extend to his beloved female: And that he is capable of being actuated by revenge, founded on fome degree of reafoning, concerning her conjugal in-fidelity. An incident, which lately happened, at the feat of Mr. B******, near Berwick, juftifies this remark. " My mowers," fays he, " cut a par-" tridge on her neft, and immediately " brought the eggs (fourteen) to the " houfe. I ordered them to be put un-" der a very large beautiful hen, and her " own to be taken away. They were " hatched in two days, and the hen " brought them up perfectly well till " they were five or fix weeks old. Du-" ring that time they were conftantly " kept confined in an outhoufe, without " having been feen by any of the other " poultry. The door happened to be left " open, and the cock got in. My houfe-

S " keeper,

" keeper, hearing her hen in diſtreſs,
" ran to her aſſiſtance, but did not arrive
" in time to ſave her life. The cock,
" finding her with the brood of par-
" tridges, fell upon her with the utmoſt
" fury, and put her to death. The
" houſe-keeper found him tearing her
" both with his beak and ſpurs, although
" ſhe was then fluttering in the laſt
" agony, and incapable of any reſiſtance.
" The hen had been, formerly, the cock's
" greateſt favourite."

A writer, of no inconſiderable merit,* has employed his muſe, on a ſubject highly intereſting to the Engliſh reader, in a didactic poem entitled the *Fleece*. In this work, whatever relates to the management of *ſheep*, and the manufac-ture of wool, is largely diſcuſſed; and the whole is adorned by the introduction of rural imagery, and amuſing digreſ-

* Mr. Dyer.

ſions.

fions. But the performance might have been rendered much more entertaining, if it had comprehended a fuller account of the natural hiftory of the fheep; and had difplayed a nicer attention to the peculiar and pleafing character of that innocent animal, and of her fportive offspring. One fact fhould not have been omitted, in fuch a narrative; and I wonder it efcaped Mr. Dyer's obfervation. I am informed, that, after the dam has been fhorn, and turned into the fold to her lambs, they become eftranged to her, and that a fcene of reciprocal dif-trefs enfues; which a man, of lively imagination, and tender feelings, might render highly interefting and pathetic. The poor fheep, when undergoing the operation of wafhing, and alfo when ftripped of her warm and graceful cover-ing is, in both circumftances a fpectacle, of pity, and a proper object of poetical amplification. Had Mr. Sterne been the

S 2

author

author of the Fleece, he would perhaps have introduced the following little epifode. "Dear Senfibility! thou fome-
" times infpireft the rough peafant, who
" traverfes the bleakeft mountains.—He
" finds the lacerated lamb of another's
" flock. This moment I beheld him,
" leaning his head againft his crook,
" with piteous inclination looking down
" upon it.—Oh! had I come one mo-
" ment fooner!—It bleeds to death.—
" His gentle heart bleeds with it.—Peace
" to thee, generous fwain! I fee thou
" walkeft off with anguifh; but thy joys
" fhall balance it. For happy is thy
" cottage;—and happy is the fharer of
" it;—and happy are the lambs, which
" fport about thee!"

SMOKE, iffuing from the chimney of a retired cottage, fhaded with trees, is a pleafing object. The waving line of beauty, in which it gradually afcends,

and

and the fucceffion of graceful forms, which it affumes, before it is loft in the atmofphere, adapts it to poetical defcription or comparifon, as well as to the canvas of the painter. Mr. Dyer, in the poem above referred to, has thus reprefented its appearance, and affociated with it· ideas of comfort and plenty, which tend to heighten the complacency of the beholder.

> Yet your mild homefteads, ever blooming fmile
> Among embracing woods, and waft on high
> The breath of plenty, from the ruddy tops
> Of chimneys, curling o'er the gloomy trees,
> In airy, azure ringlets, to the fky. *

The FLOATING MISTS, which are feen on the tops and fides of hills, often put on a variety of agreeable fhapes and colours. They conftitute an interefting part of the fcenery of Offian's poems;

* Dyer's Fleece, Book I. line 509.

and

and are introduced, with peculiar propriety, as objects which, in a mountainous country, were continually within
the view of his *dramatis perſonæ.* " The
" miſt of Cromla curls upon the rock,
" and ſhines to the beam of the weſt.
" The ſoft miſt pours over the ſilent vale.
" The green flowers are filled with dew.
" The ſun returns in his ſtrength; and
" the miſt is gone." Theſe beautiful
forms ſuggeſt, to a devout mind, converſant with the writings of Milton, part
of Adam's morning invocation.

> Ye miſts and exhalations, that now riſe
> From hill or ſteaming lake, duſky or grey,
> Till the ſun paint your fleecy ſkirts with gold,
> In honour to the world's great Author riſe,
> Whether to deck with clouds th' uncoloured ſky,
> Or wet the thirſty earth with falling ſhowers,
> Riſing or falling, ſtill advance his praiſe. *

The expreſſion *ſteaming lake,* in the ſecond
line, is uſed with the ſtricteſt philoſophical

* Milton, Book V.

trtuh

truth. Thomson has applied the same epithet, with equal justness, to that intestine motion in the earth, by which Divine Providence

Works in the secret deep, shoots *steaming* thence
The fair profusion, that o'erspreads the spring.

For it appears, from some late experiments, that sixteen hundred gallons of water rise, by evaporation, from an acre of ground, within the space of twelve hours, of a summer's day.*

An inattentive observer of nature would hardly remark the CURVILINEAR DIRECTION, in the motion of animals. Yet certain it is, that neither birds, fishes, insects, quadrupeds, nor men, ever move long in a straight line. The final cause of this seems to be, that ease may be alternately given to the muscles, on the

* Watson's Chemical Essays, Vol. III. p. 52.

 right

right and on the left fide of the body.
When the mufcles of the right fide are
in a ftate of vigorous exertion, the direction of the body will incline that way;
and when they require relief, thofe of the
left fide come into action, and produce
an oppofite effect. Whoever follows a
draught horfe heavily laden, will perceive
the truth of this obfervation. And it is
not more apparent on the beaten high-
way, than in the fheep-tracks on the
heath, and in the paths, worn by the
paffage of cattle to their watering places.
Hence it is a rule, in the art of gardening,
that walks and pleafure grounds fhould
be ferpentine; as that form is moft
agreeable to nature, and therefore moft
confonant to an elegant and improved
tafte.

Milton makes frequent mention of the
FLAMING SWORDS, borne by the angelic
fpirits, and particularly by the cheru-
bims,

bims, who were ftationed at the gate of Paradife.

> And on the eaft fide of the garden place,
> Where entrance up from Eden eafieft climbs,
> Cherubic watch ; and of a fword, the flame
> Wide waving, all approach far off to fright,
> And guard all paffage to the tree of life. *

If the Poet had been acquainted with the modern difcoveries in electricity, he might perhaps have feized this occafion of exerting his fuperior talents for defcription, by a more minute and pictorial difplay of *the fword of flame wide waving.* The reader, at leaft, may affift his imagination to conceive a more lively idea of it, by the following beautiful experiment.

Make a torricellian *vacuum*, in a glafs tube, about three feet long, and feal it

* Paradife Loft, Book XI. line 120.

hermetically.

hermetically.   Let one end of this tube
be held in the hand, and the other applied to the electrical conductor; and
immediately the whole tube will be il-
luminated, and when taken from the
conductor, will continue luminous for a
confiderable time.   If it be then drawn
through the hand, the light will be un-
commonly intenfe, from end to end, without the leaft interruption.   After this
operation, which difcharges it in a great
meafure, it will ftill flafh at intervals,
though held only at one extremity, and
quite ftill.   But if it be grafped by the
other hand, at the fame time, in a different place, ftrong flafhes of light will
dart from one extremity to the other,
and continue to do fo twenty-four hours,
or perhaps longer, without frefh ex-
citation. *

* See Dr. Prieftley's Hift. of Electricity, p. 540.

The

The foregoing experiment was made by Mr. Canton, to elucidate the nature of the Aurora Borealis, a phenomenon well fuited to exercife the fancy of the poet. But ftill more congenial to him are thofe illufive meteors, which fome-times occur in northern climates; and which, literally, give " to airy nothing a local habitation and a name."   " I was " never more furprifed," fays Crantz, in his Hiftory of Greenland, " than on a " fine warm fummer's day, to perceive " the iflands, that lie four leagues weft " of our fhore, putting on a form quite " different from what they are known " to have. As I ftood gazing upon them, " they appeared at firft infinitely greater " than what they naturally are ; and " feemed as if I viewed them through " a large magnifying glafs. They were " thus not only made larger, but brought " nearer to me: I plainly defcried every " ftone upon the land, and all the furrows
" filled

" filled with ice. When this deception
" had lasted for a while, the prospect
" seemed to break up, and a new scene
" of wonder to present itself. The islands
" seemed to travel to the shore, and
" represented a wood, or a tall cut hedge.
" The scene then shifted, and shewed
" the appearance of all sorts of curious
" figures; as ships with sails, streamers,
" and flags, antique elevated castles with
" decayed turrets; and a thousand forms,
" for which fancy found a resemblance
" in nature. When the eye had been
" satisfied with gazing, the whole group
" seemed to rise in air, and at length
" vanish into nothing. At such times,
" the air is quite serene and clear;
" but comprest with subtle vapours; and
" these, appearing between the eye and
" the object, give it all that variety of
" appearances, which glasses, of different
" refrangibilities, would have done."*

* See Goldsmith's History of the Earth, Vol. I.

However

However marvellous this narrative may appear to a phlegmatic reader, it will not seem incredible to the poet, whose fancy can form a still brighter, and more gay creation, without the aid of aerial refractions or reflections. And if these fictions deviate not too far from verisimilitude, they agreeably agitate the mind with the mixed emotions of surprise and delight. But, in delineations of nature, they have no legitimate place; and the judgment rejects, with disgust, whatever falsifies the truth of description, by its obvious incongruity. Myrtle groves, perennial springs, unfading flowers, and odoriferous gales, the hackneyed Arcadian scenery, accord not with an English landscape. And equally unsuitable, to the views of this country, are the spicy beauties, and pearly treasures of the East. Yet Milton, in his Comus, thus addresses the goddess of the Severn;

May

May thy billows roll afhore,
· The beryl, and the golden ore!
May thy lofty head be crown'd
With many a tower, and terrace round;
And here and there, thy banks upon,
With groves of myrrh and cinnamon.

But the poet is not, upon all occafions, to be confined within the precife boundaries of truth. What writer, of lively fancy, in defcribing a morning walk on the banks of Kefwick, would not embellifh the beauty of the fcene by introducing the MELODY OF BIRDS; and thus add the charms of mufic to all the enchantments of vifion. Yet, I believe, there is not a feathered fongfter to be found in thofe delightful vales; probably, owing to the terror infpired by the birds of prey, which abound on the mountains that furround them. At Grange, about four miles from the lake, there is an eagle's eyrie. The neft is circular, compofed of twigs twifted together;

gether; and is more than a yard in diameter. The eagles, which inhabit it, are of the species called the erne, or the vulture Albicilla, of Linnæus. And they are said to commit great destruction amongst the hares, partridges, grouse, and even lambs of that district.*

I cannot close this Essay, without making an apology for the freedom of my strictures on poetical demerit. And I feel a peculiar diffidence with respect to my animadversions on a poet, who is justly the boast and glory of Britain. To pluck a leaf from the brow of Milton, may be deemed a sacrilegious attempt to injure the laurels of our country: But it should be recollected, that error is most dangerous, when dignified by high example; and that it is no disparagement to genius, however exalted,

* See Mr. Gray's Tour to the Lakes.

to afcribe to it, fome portion of that imperfection, which is the common allotment of humanity.

A

TRIBUTE

TO THE MEMORY OF

CHARLES DE POLIER, Esq;

ADDRESSED TO THE

LITERARY AND PHILOSOPHICAL SOCIETY OF MANCHESTER.

T

OCTOBER 30th, 1782.

AT a meeting of the LITERARY AND PHILO-SOPHICAL SOCIETY of MANCHESTER, *the following resolution passed unanimously.*

" *The Members of the* LITERARY AND PHILO-SOPHICAL SOCIETY *lamenting, with heartfelt concern, the death of their late much honoured brother,* CHARLES DE POLIER, *Esq; unanimously resolve, that* DR. PERCIVAL *be requested to draw up a grateful and respectful Tribute to his Memory; to be inserted in the journals of the Society, with a view to record his distinguished merit, and to prolong the influence of his bright example.*"

NOVEMBER 13th, 1782.

At a meeting of the LITERARY AND PHILO-SOPHICAL SOCIETY, *it was resolved unanimously,* " *That the Thanks of the Society be returned to* DR. PERCIVAL, *for his Tribute to the Memory of* CHARLES DE POLIER, *Esq; and that he be desired to print the same.*"

A

TRIBUTE to the MEMORY

OF

CHARLES DE POLIER, Esq;

ADDRESSED TO THE

LITERARY AND PHILOSOPHICAL SOCIETY
OF MANCHESTER.

THE contemplation of moral and intellectual excellence affords the moſt pleaſing and inſtructive exerciſe, to a well conſtituted mind. By exalting our ideas of the human character, it expands and heightens the principle of benevolence; and at the ſame time is favourable to piety, by raiſing our views to the ſupreme Author of all that is fair and good in man. The wiſe and the virtuous have ever dwelt, with delight, on the meritorious talents and diſpoſitions of their fellow-creatures : And an

T 2

amiable

amiable philofopher drew, from this fource, fuch fweet confolations, under the toils and diftreffes of life, that he warmly recommends the practice to our imitation. *" When you would recreate " yourfelf,"* fays M. Antoninus, *" reflect " on the laudable qualities of your acquaint- " ance: On the magnanimity of one, the " modefty of another, or the liberality of a " third."** Generous meditation! which every one, prefent, may indulge; and, by indulging, affimilate, to his own nature, the various perfections of others; transfufing, as it were, into his breaft, the virtues which he contemplates.

But can we engage ourfelves in fuch an exercife, without the moft lively recollection of our late honoured and beloved colleague? His image prefents itfelf before us; and we inftantly recognife the agreeablenefs of his form, the animation of his countenance, the vigour of

* M. Antonin. Lib. VI.

his

his underftanding, and the goodnefs of his heart. How graceful was his addrefs; how fprightly, entertaining, and intelligent his converfation! What rich ftores of knowledge did he difplay; what facility in the ufe, what judgment in the application of them! Few have been the fubjects of difcuffion in this Society, which his obfervations have not enlightened: And what he could not himfelf elucidate, he has enabled others to do, by the pertinency of his queries, and the fagacity of his conjectures. So quick was his penetration; fo enlarged his comprehenfion; fo exact the arrangement of his intellectual treafures! Learning, with fome, is the parent of mental obfcurity; and the multiplicity of ideas, which have been acquired by fevere ftudy, ferve only to produce perplexity and confufion. But Mr. de Polier's thoughts were always ready at command. And he engaged, with perfpicuity, on every topic of difcourfe; becaufe he faw,

T 3

at

at one view, all its relations and analogies
to thofe branches of knowledge, with
which he was already acquainted. With
fuch felicity of genius, he was continually
making large acceffions to his ftock of
fcience, without laborious refearches, or
feclufion from the focial enjoyments of
life.

Of his abilities as a writer, he furnifhed us with a ftriking proof, in the
Differtation he delivered, laft winter;*
which is equally diftinguifhed by the
juftnefs of its fentiments, and the purity
of its diction; and fully difplays his perfect attainment, both of the idiom and
embellifhments of the Englifh language.

But Mr. de Polier had merits, more
eftimable than thofe, which he derived
from the vivacity of his fancy, the elegance of his tafte, or the powers of his

* On the pleafure which the mind receives, from the *exercife*
of its faculties, and particularly that of *tafte.*

under-

understanding. And his friends will cordially unite with me in testifying, that, if honoured for his *intellectual*, he was beloved for his *moral* endowments. His heart was open to every generous sympathy; and the sensibility of his nature so enlivened all his perceptions, that the ordinary duties of social intercourse were performed, by him, with a warmth, almost equal to that of friendship. Nor was this the artificial deportment of unmeaning courtesy; but the generous effusion of a heart, which felt for all mankind. In such *philanthropy*, politeness has its true foundation: And of this joint grace of nature and education, " which aids and strengthens Virtue " where it meets her, and imitates her " actions, where she is not," our lamented brother was a bright example. So engaging were his manners, and at the same time so sincere his disposition, that we may apply to him, with *honour*, what Cicero meant as a *reproach*; that

T 4

he

he was qualified, *cum triftibus fevére, cum remiffis jucunde, cum fenibus graviter, cum juventute comiter vivere.* Thefe powers of pleafing flowed from no fervile compliances, nor ever led him into criminal indulgences. As a companion, he was convivial without intemperance, and gay without levity or licentioufnefs. His converfation was fprightly and unreferved; but, in the moft unguarded hours of mirth, exempt from all indecency and profanenefs. And the fallies of his wit and pleafantry were fo feafoned with good humour, that they gave delight, unmixed with pain, even to thofe who were the objects of them. If the coarfer pleafures of the bottle be banifhed from our tables; or if rational converfation, and delicacy of behaviour, with the fweet fociety of the fofter fex, be now fubftituted in their room, this happy revolution has been rendered more complete by the influence of Mr. de Polier.

But

But though URBANITY, according to the moſt liberal interpretation of that term, was the *characteriſtic* of our excellent colleague, he poſſeſſed other endowments, of more intrinſic value. And I could enlarge, with pleaſure, on his nice ſenſe of rectitude, his inviolable integrity, and ſacred regard to truth. Theſe moral virtues were, in him, founded on no fictitious principle of *honour*, but reſulted from the conſtitution of his mind; and were ſtrengthened by habit, regulated by reaſon, and ſanctioned by religion. For, notwithſtanding, the veil which he choſe to caſt over his *piety*, it was manifeſt to his intimate friends; and may be recollected by others, who have marked the ſerioufneſs, with which he diſcourſed, on every ſubject relative to the being and attributes of GOD. Defective indeed muſt be the character of that man, who can diſcern and acknowledge, without venerating the divine perfections; and partake of

the

the bounties of nature, yet feel no emotions of gratitude towards its benevolent
Author.   "*A little philosophy,*" says lord
Verulam, "*may incline the mind to atheism;*
"*but depth in philosophy will bring it about*
"*again to religion.*"*

I have thus attempted to draw a rude
sketch of the features, of our late honoured friend. A fuller delineation might
furnish a more pleasing picture to strangers.; but, to the members of this society, a few outlines will suffice to revive
the image of the beloved original.   This
image, I trust, will be long and forcibly
impressed on our minds; and that every
one, here present, may adopt the language of Tacitus, on a similar occasion.
"*Quicquid ex Agricola amavimus, quicquid*

---

* The noble author subjoins a just reason, for this observation. "For while the mind of man," says he, "looketh upon
"*second causes* scattered, it may sometimes rest in them, and
"go no farther: But when it beholdeth the chain of them
"linked together, it must needs fly to Providence and Deity."
BACON's Essay on Atheism.

"*mirati*

" mirati fumus, manet, manfurumque eft in
" animis hominum."   " Whatever in
" Agricola was the object of our love
" and of our admiration, remains, and
" will remain, in the hearts of all who
" knew him."

Having taken a fhort view of the
character of Mr. de Polier, curiofity and
attachment concur in prompting us, to
extend the retrofpect; and we become
folicitous to know fomething of his connections and education; and to trace the
leading events of a life, in the conclufion
of which we have been fo deeply in-
terefted. But our friend was no egotift;
and the zeal with which he entered into
the concerns of others, precluded the
detail of his own. I muft content myfelf, therefore, with prefenting to the
fociety, the following brief memoirs.

Charles de Polier Bottens was the fon
of the Reverend —— de Polier Bottens,
Dean

Dean of the Cathedral Church of Laufanne, Prefident of the Synod of the Pais de Vaud, Member of the Society of Arts and Sciences at Manheim, and citizen of Geneva. He was born at Laufanne, in the year 1753; and received the firft part of his education, in the public fchools of that city. As foon as he had acquired a fufficient knowledge of the claffics, he was fent to an academy near Caffel, in Germany; from whence, after a refidence of two years, he was removed to the univerfity of Gottingen. In this celebrated feat of learning, he paffed three years; and being then inclined to a military life, he obtained a lieutenant's commiffion in the Swifs regiment of D'Erlact, in the French fervice. But he foon refigned his commiffion, and returned to Laufanne; where he had a command given him, in one of the Provincial regiments of dragoons. In this fituation, his connection commenced with the Earl of Tyrone; who offered him the tuition of his eldeft fon,

Lord

Lord le Poer, on terms equally honourable and advantageous. But before the engagement was completed, propofals were made to him by the duke of Saxe Gotha, to become governor to the hereditary prince, with an annuity, for life, of twelve hundred rixdollars; an apartment at court; and the poft of chamberlain, or rank of colonel. Thefe propofals, however, he declined in favour of lord Tyrone. And he executed the important truft, affigned to him, with fuch judgment, tendernefs, and fidelity, as induced that refpectable nobleman to commit three of his children to his fole direction. Thefe amiable youths he brought to England, in the fummer of 1779; and fettled them at the fchool of a clergyman in Manchefter, who is eminently diftinguifhed by his virtues as a man, and abilities as a teacher.

At this period, our firft acquaintance with Mr. de Polier was formed. By

the

the laws of hofpitality, he was entitled to our attention, as a ftranger. But his perfonal accomplifhments, and the charms of his converfation, foon fuperfeded the ordinary claims of cuftom, and converted formal civility into efteem and friendfhip. He became our companion in pleafure; our affiftant in ftudy; our counfellor in difficulty; and our folace in diftrefs. Amufement acquired a dignity and zeft, by his participation; and he foftened the aufterity of philofophy, whenever he joined in the purfuit. The inftitution, which now celebrates his memory, owes to him much of its popularity and fuccefs; and, fo long as it fubfifts, his name will be revered, as one of its founders and moft fhining ornaments.

About the middle of laft winter he was attacked by a complaint, which at firft gave no difturbance to the vital functions. But being aggravated by the

fatigues

fatigues of a long journey to Holyhead, and of a voyage from thence to Dublin, at a time when he laboured under the *Influenza*, his malady rapidly increased after his arrival in Ireland; and put a final period to his valuable life on the 18th of October 1782.* The vigour of his faculties, and the warmth of his affections, continued even to the hour of his diffolution. And the amiableness of his behaviour, in the clofing fcene of trial and fuffering through which he paffed, gave fuch completion to his character, that we may apply to him, what the Poet has faid of Mr. Addifon;

--- He taught us how to live; and, oh! too high
The price of knowledge, taught us how to die.†

On this affecting event, I cannot exprefs your feelings and my own, in terms fo forcible as thofe of the animated hif-

---

* At CURRAGHMORE, near WATERFORD, the feat of the Earl of Tyrone.

† Tickell's Poem on the Death of Addifon.

torian,

torian, whom I have before quoted. *Si quis piorum manibus locus; si, ut sapientibus placet, non cum corpore exstinguuntur magnæ animæ; placide quiescas, nosque ab infirmo desiderio, ad contemplationem virtutum tuarum voces, quas neque lugeri, neque plangi fas est! Admiratione te potius temporalibus laudibus, et si natura suppeditet, militum decoramus!** "If there be any "habitation for the shades of the virtu- "ous; if, as philosophers suppose, ex- "alted souls do not perish with the body; "may you repose in peace, and recall "us from vain regret, to the contem- "plation of your virtues, which allow "no place for mourning or complaint! "Let us adorn your memory, rather, "by a fixed admiration, and, if our "natures will permit, by an imitation "of your excellent qualities, than by "temporary eulogies!" †

* Tacit. Vit. Agricolæ.

† See Mr. Aikin's Translation of the Life of Agricola.

A N

AN APPENDIX

TO THE

SOCRATIC DISCOURSE;

CONTAINING

SUPPLEMENTARY REMARKS,

AND ILLUSTRATIONS.

U

ADVERTISEMENT.

As the Socratic mode of discussion admits not of interruption by notes, the author has chosen to insert, in this place, such additional REMARKS and ILLUSTRATIONS, concerning the subject matter of the discourse on TRUTH, as further reading or reflection have suggested to his mind.

A N

A P P E N D I X

T O   T H E

S O C R A T I C   D I S C O U R S E;

C O N T A I N I N G

SUPPLEMENTARY REMARKS,

AND ILLUSTRATIONS.

I. TRUE AND FALSE HONOUR.[*]

THERE is a principle of HONOUR, which seems to be, in some measure, distinct from that of virtue, and originates from the association of certain ideas of propriety, or pride, with rectitude of conduct. Amongst the ancient

[*] See page 11.

U 2   Greeks

Greeks and Romans, Virtue and Honour were deified; and a joint altar was confecrated to them at Rome. But afterwards each of them had feparate temples; fo connected, however, that no one could enter the temple of honour, without paffing through that of virtue.

The genuine principle of honour, in its full extent, may be defined, a quick perception, and lively feeling of moral obligation, particularly with refpect to probity and truth, in conjunction with an acute fenfibility to fhame, reproach, or infamy. But in different characters, thefe two conftituent parts of the principle are found to exift in proportions fo widely diverfified, as, fometimes, to appear almoft fingle and detached. The former always *aids and ftrengthens virtue*; the latter may, occafionally, *imitate her actions,* * when fafhion happily countenances,

* Honour's a facred tie, the law of kings,
  The noble mind's diftinguifhing perfection,

That

nances, or high example prompts to rectitude. But being connected, for the most part, with a jealous pride, and capricious irritability, it will be more shocked with the *imputation*, than with the *commission* of what is wrong. And thus it will conftitute that fpurious honour, which, by a perverfion of the laws of affociation, *puts evil for good, and good for evil*; and, under the fanction of a name, perpetrates crimes without remorfe, and even without ignominy. To this empirical morality *duelling* owes its rife, which, with a fatal confidence, pretends to cure the indecorums of focial intercourfe, whilft it deftroys the lives of individuals, fubverts the peace of families, and violates the moft facred laws of the community. It is aftonifhing that a practice, which originated in the dark ages of ignorance,

That aids and ftrengthens Virtue where it meets her,
And imitates her actions where fhe is not:
It ought not to be fported with.
ADDISON's Cato.

U 3   fuperfti-

superstition, and disorder, should be continued in this enlightened period, though condemned by the polity of every state, and utterly repugnant to the spirit, and precepts of Christianity. The ancient Germans, Danes, and Franks, were used to decide criminal questions of fact, in the last resort, by combat. But this method of trial, about the close of the fifth century, was restrained to the following conditions. 1. That the crime, for which it was instituted, should be capital. 2. That it should be certain, that the crime had been perpetrated. 3. That the accused, by common fame, should be supposed guilty. 4. That the matter should not be capable of proof by witnesses. A custom, thus regulated, appears wise and equitable, in comparison with modern duelling, which has seldom any object, but the redress of fantastic wrongs, or the display of resentment, that often subsides before its execution. Is there a man of probity and humanity,

and

and many of this character, I am perfuaded, have been feduced by the illu-
fions of falfe honour, who, if not pro-
hibited by law, would think himfelf authorifed to call forth his antagonift, place
him as a mark, and appoint a ruffian to
fire a piftol at him, becaufe, in the heat
of argument, or in the unguarded hours
of convivial mirth, he has committed
fome trifling offence, or verbal incivility?
And is it not adding the moft egregious
folly to injuftice, to undertake himfelf
this opprobrious office, at the hazard of
his own life, and to the ruin, perhaps,
of his deareft connections? For, I pre-
fume, it now forms no part of the creed
of the duellift, that Divine Providence
will interpofe, on fuch occafions, to
preferve the injured, and to punifh the
aggreffor.

The military fpirit, which a long war
has revived amongft the inhabitants of
this country, and which the armed affo-
U 4

ciations

ciations, eftablifhed in different places, cannot fail to fofter and fupport, may, perhaps, contribute to multiply challenges, and to extend the practice of fingle combat. Courage is fo effential to the character of a foldier, that it becomes magnified in his eftimation, far beyond its real defert: And he is not only in danger of miftaking its true nature, and proper object, but of acquiring a contempt for every virtue, which, in his perverted judgment, ftands in competition with it. Like Achilles, *jura negat fibi nata; nihil non arrogat armis.* Reafon and religion fhould, therefore, exert their united authority, to check the influence of fuch baneful errors: And law fhould rigoroufly punifh, with difgrace and infamy, the man, who can facrifice humanity to pride, and juftice to the fpecious counterfeit of gallantry.

I fhall clofe this fection with the following paffage, from the celebrated Commen-

Commentaries of Sir William Blackstone.
" Exprefs malice is, when one, with a
" fedate, deliberate mind, and formed
" defign, doth kill another; which formed
" defign is evidenced by external cir-
" cumftances difcovering that inward
" intention; as, lying in wait, antecedent
" menaces, former grudges, and con-
" certed fchemes to do him fome bodily
" harm.   This takes in the cafe of deli-
" berate duelling, where both parties
" meet, avowedly, with an intent to
" murder; thinking it their duty as
" gentlemen, and claiming it as their
" right, to wanton with their own lives,
" and thofe of their fellow-creatures;
" without any warrant or authority, from
" any power, either human or divine,
" but in direct contradiction to the laws
" both of God and man : And there-
" fore, the law has juftly fixed the crime
" and punifhment of murder, on them,
" and on their feconds alfo." *

* Book IV. Chap. 14.

II. FALSE

II. FALSE MAXIMS OF MORALITY.*

THE hiſtory of Lord Herbert, of Cherbury, admirably exemplifies the folly and danger of adopting FALSE MAXIMS of MORALITY. From the variety of inſtances, which offer themſelves, in the memoirs of this romantic nobleman, I ſhall ſelect the following. During his abode at the duke of Montmorency's, about twenty-four miles from Paris, it happened, one evening, that a daughter of the dutchefs de Ventadour, of about ten or eleven years of age, went to walk in the meadows with his lordſhip, and ſeveral other gentlemen and ladies. The young lady wore a knot of ribband on her head, which a French chevalier ſnatched away, and faſtened to his hat-band. He was deſired to return it, but

* See page 13.

refuſed.

refused. The lady then requested lord Herbert to recover it for her. A race ensued; and the chevalier, finding himself likely to be overtaken, made a sudden turn, and was about to deliver his prize to the young lady, when lord Herbert seized his arm, and cried out, " I give it you." " Pardon me," said the lady, " it is he who gives it me." " Madam," replied lord Herbert, " I " will not contradict you; but if the " chevalier do not acknowledge, that I " constrain him to give the ribband, " I will fight with him." And the next day he sent him a challenge, " being " bound thereunto," says he, " by the " oath taken when I was made knight " of the bath."

He relates, also, three other similar cases, to shew, *how strictly he held himself to his oath of knighthood*. " This oath," says the ingenious editor of lord Herbert's life, " is one remnant of a superstitious
" and

" and romantic age, which an age, call-
" ing itfelf enlightened, ftill retains.
" The folemn fervice at the inveftiture
" of the knights, which has not the leaft
" connection with any thing holy, is
" a piece of the fame profane pageantry.
" The oath being no longer fuppofed
" to bind, it is ftrange mockery to in-
" voke heaven on fo trifling an occafion."
And it would be more ftrange, if each
knight, like the mifguided lord Herbert,
fhould think himfelf obliged to cut a
man's throat, whenever a young lady
lofes her top-knot!

Thefe religious engagements are fo
often mifapplied, that it cannot be un-
feafonable, to enter into a brief difcuffion
of their true nature and obligation. A
vow may be defined, *a devout promife made
to* GOD, *refpecting either the performance,
or omiffion, of fome voluntary act*; and is
often accompanied with an imprecation
of Divine vengeance, on the infraction

of

of it. The only legitimate ufe of fuch
an engagement is, to increafe our abhorrence of what is evil, and to confirm
our refolution in the more arduous purfuits of virtue. It cannot, therefore,
be applied to the neglect of any antecedent duty, or to the accomplifhment
of any impious or immoral purpofe.
Were it otherwife, thefe arbitrary ties
might be made a plea for violating every
law, whether human or divine. Even
prudence, in certain cafes, is of fufficient
force to fuperfede the validity of a vow.
Thus, if the fuperftitious parent of a
numerous and helplefs family were, in
fome preffing danger, to invoke the
affiftance of Heaven, by the moft folemn
avowal of his refolution, to give all his
fubftance to the church, or to the poor;
fuch an abfurd intention has not the
nature of an engagement, and is void in
itfelf. For, we are affured, that the
execution of it could never prove acceptable to a wife and benevolent Deity,
with

with whom alone the contract was made. But this reasoning does not extend to rash and injurious bargains; or to promises of a social nature, which have been confirmed by an oath. For, as the maintenance of faith is of the highest importance in the commerce of life, to add impiety to the breach of it, must certainly be deemed an aggravation of the offence. And in such instances *the good man changeth not, though he swear to his own hurt.*

III. FEALTY TO MAGISTRATES. *

THE COMMANDS of the MAGISTRATE, or of the LEGISLATURE, are not binding, when they oppose the known and acknowledged obligations of morality. And the younger Cato has been justly censured, for engaging in the execution,

* See page 14.

of

of what he himself deemed a violent and most oppressive sentence, against Ptolemy, king of Cyprus. This prince was brother to the king of Egypt; and reigned by the same right of hereditary succession. He was in full peace and amity with Rome; and was accused of no practices, nor suspected of any designs, against the republic. But the infamous Clodius, who was then tribune, proposed and obtained the law, from motives of private pique and revenge. To give a sanction to it, Cato was charged with its fulfilment; and undertook the commission, though contrary to all his ideas of justice and rectitude. I believe no moralist, of the present times, will admit the validity of Cicero's apology, for the misconduct of his friend. " The " commission," says he, " was designed " not to adorn, but to banish Cato; " not offered, but imposed upon him. " Why then did he obey it? For the " same reason, that he *swore to obey*

" other

" other laws, which he knew to be un-
" juſt; that he might not expoſe himſelf
" to the fury of his enemies, or, by a
" fruitleſs pertinacity, deprive the re-
" public of his ſervices." *Orat. pro
Sexto.*

The conduct of SCIPIO AFRICANUS, in
the deſtruction of the brave Numantines,
is equally reprehenſible. For it is confeſſed, by Lucius Florus, that the
Romans commenced hoſtilities againſt
that people, without even a pretence to
render them juſtifiable. And the horrid
barbarities, exerciſed in the ſiege of
Numantia, excite peculiar indignation,
from the unparalleled fortitude and vigour, which the inhabitants diſplayed,
in the defence of their liberties. Such
bravery, exerted in a cauſe ſo noble,
merited the patronage, and ſhould have
called forth the clemency, not the reſent-
ment, of Scipio. But the Romans appear
to have entertained no conſiſtent ideas,

concerning

concerning the privileges of other nations, or the common rights of mankind.
They proudly arrogated to themselves
the government of the world; and the
maxim, *regere imperio populos,** was the
plea for every conqueſt. This principle
pervades the writings of all their poets
and hiſtorians: And even the philoſophical TACITUS, in delivering the memoirs of Agricola, expreſſes not the
ſlighteſt diſapprobation, of the numerous, and deſtructive expeditions into
Britain. Yet he has, inadvertently, put
into the mouth of Galgacus, one of the
chieftains of our warlike anceſtors, ſuch
ſentiments, as may be deemed a ſtigma
on his venerable father-in-law, for
obedience to imperial mandates, founded on cruelty and injuſtice. *Raptores
orbis, poſtquam cuncta vaſtantibus defuere,
terra, et mare ſcrutantur: Si locuples hoſtis*

* *Tu,* REGERE IMPERIO POPULOS, *Romane memento,*
(*Hæ tibi erunt artes*) *pacifque imponere morem,*
Parcere ſubjectis, et debellare ſuperbos. VIRG.

X   *eſt,*

*eſt, avari; ſi pauper, ambitioſi. Quos non oriens, non occidens ſatiaverit : Soli omnium, opes atque inopiam, pari affeƐtu concupiſcunt. Auferre, trucidare, rapere falſis nominibus, imperium; atque ubi ſolitudinem faciunt, pacem apellant.**

" Theſe plunderers of the world, after
" exhauſting the land by their devaſ-
" tations, are rifling the ocean: ſtimu-
" lated by avarice, if their enemy be
" rich; by ambition, if poor: Unſa-
" tiated by the eaſt, and by the weſt:
" The only people, who behold wealth
" and indigence with equal avidity: To
" ravage, to ſlaughter, to uſurp, under
" falſe titles, they call empire: And when
" they make a deſart, they call it peace."†

Modern conqueſts have been founded on claims equally invalid and tyrannical, with thoſe of the Romans. It is a ſatire

---

* Tacit. Vit. Agric.

† Aikin's Tranſlation of the Life of Agricola.

on

on human reafon, and ftill more difgraceful to the moral feelings of mankind, to review the principles, on which the Spaniards affected to eftablifh their rights to the extenfive dominions in the new world. Their generals were inftructed to notify, with great formality, to the innocent and ignorant natives of the weftern hemifphere, that St. Peter had fubjected the univerfe to the jurifdiction of the Roman Pontiff; and that this lord of the whole creation had made a grant of the iflands, of the *Terra Firma,* and of the ocean, to the Catholic Kings of Caftile. To thefe monarchs they were required to fubject themfelves; and, if they refufed, the moft exemplary vengeance was denounced againft them. They were threatened to be defpoiled of their wives and children, to have their country ravaged, and to be themfelves fold for flaves.*

* See Herrara, Dec. I. Lib. 7, Cap. 14. alfo Robertfon's Hiftory of America, note 23.

X 2

Inftances,

Inftances, like thefe, afford the moft irrefragable evidence, that fealty to ma-giftrates muft always be regarded, as a conditional obligation; and that implicit obedience to their commands may in-volve us in high degrees of guilt and infamy.

IV. FALSE OPINIONS CONCERNING FRIENDSHIP.*

MANY of the ancients appear to have entertained very enthufiaftic notions of FRIENDSHIP; and to have fup-pofed, that it fuperfedes, in particular circumftances, both wifdom and pru-dence, and every fpecies of moral obli-gation.   When Bloffius, the bofom com-panion of the elder Gracchus, was fum-moned before the fenate of Rome, after the tumult which proved fatal to that tribune, he was interrogated, whether

* See page 19.

he

he had always obeyed the commands of
Gracchus? "Yes," anſwered Bloſſius,
" moſt punctually, for ſo I thought it
" my duty to do. And, if it had been
" poſſible for him to deſire me to fire
" the Capitol, I ſhould not have ſcrupled
" to comply, from my full confidence in
" his rectitude."* The folly and criminality of ſuch a blind ſacrifice of reaſon
and judgment to the will of another,
are too obvious to need any comment.
Connections, of this ſervile nature, merit
not the honourable appellation of friendſhip. And we may juſtly adopt the
opinion, which Cicero has delivered,
concerning them: *Si omnia facienda ſint,
quæ amici velint, non* AMICITIÆ *tales ſed*
CONJURATIONES *putandæ ſunt.*†

Not leſs foreign to the true obligations
of this amiable and venerable paſſion,

* Plut. Vit. Gracchi.　　　† Cic. de Off.
- - - - - - - - - - The friendſhips of the world
Are oft *confederacies* in vice.　ADDISON's Cato.

X 3

was

was the exclamation of Themiſtocles :
" God forbid, that I ſhould ſit upon a
" tribunal, where my friends were not
" more favoured than ſtrangers !"   The
letter of king Ageſilaus, to one of the
Spartan judges, which Plutarch has pre-
ſerved, is a ſtill more ſtriking proof of
the practical influence of the ſame falſe
opinion ; becauſe this prince was a man
of probity and equity, virtues which
belonged not to the Athenian ſtateſmen.
" If Nicias be innocent," ſays he, " acquit
" him, for the ſake of juſtice ; but, if he
" be guilty, acquit him, for the ſake of
" my attachment to him."*   The Roman
moraliſt, whom I have ſo lately quoted,
very forcibly objects to the interference
of friendſhip, in the magiſterial functions :
Yet, by a ſtrange deluſion, he permits
an advocate to give a *plauſible colouring*
to the offence, with which his friend is
charged ; and to place the fact in the

* Plut. in Vit. Ageſilai.

moſt

moft advantageous, though it fhould be a *falfe* light.* In his treatife *de Amicitia,* he remarks, that, " in cafes, which affect " the life, or good fame of a friend, it " may be allowable to deviate, a little, " from what is *ftrictly right,* in order to " comply with his defires ; provided, " however, that our own character be " not injured by it." Such loofe and erroneous maxims certainly merit animadverfion. And I fhall relate the following incident, which occurred feveral centuries before the period of Cicero, as an antidote to them. Chilo, the Lacedemonian, one of the fages of Greece, who is celebrated for the fentence, KNOW THYSELF, which he caufed to be written, at Delphos, in letters of gold, is faid to have addreffed himfelf to his friends, when on his death bed, in terms to this effect. " I cannot, through the courfe " of a long life, look back, with uneafi-

* Cic. de Off. Lib. II. 14.

X 4

" nefs,

" nefs, upon any fingle inftance of my
" conduct, unlefs, perhaps, on that, which
" I am going to mention, wherein, I
" confefs, I am ftill doubtful, whether
" I acted properly or not. I was once
" appointed judge, in conjunction with
" two others, when my particular friend
" was arraigned before us. Were the
" laws to have taken their due courfe,
" he muft, inevitably, have been con-
" demned to die. After much debate,
" therefore, with myfelf, I adopted this
" expedient. I gave my own vote, ac-
" cording to my confcience, but, at the
" fame time, employed all my eloquence
" to prevail with my affociates to abfolve
" the criminal. Now I cannot but re-
" flect upon this act, with concern, from
" an apprehenfion, that there was fome-
" thing of perfidy, in perfuading others
" to go counter to what I myfelf efteemed
" right." *

* See fome judicious obfervations on this fubject, in Fitz-
ofborne's Letters.

Tully's

Tully's falfe ideas, concerning the privileges of friendfhip, betrayed him on feveral occafions, into meannefs, and even immorality of conduct. In one of his letters, he earneftly folicits Atticus, to be guilty of prevarication, in his defence. It feems that he had written an invective oration, againft an eminent fenator, fuppofed to be Curio. The piece was defigned only for the entertainment of a felect party; but had fallen into the hands of his enemies, and been publifhed by them. He wrote, therefore, to his friend, in the following terms. *Percuffifti autem me de oratione prolata; cui vulneri, ut fcribis, medere, fi quid potes.* ——— *et, quia fcripta mihi videtur negligentius, quam cæteræ, puto poffes probare non effe meam.* * " You have " fhocked me with the news that my " oration is made public. Heal the " wound, if you poffibly can. ———

* Ep. ad Attic. III. 12.

" As

"As it is written more negligently than "my other orations, I think you may "prove it *not to be mine.*" It is remarkable, that Tully fhould have made a requeft, of this nature, to Atticus, who is faid to have had fuch an abhorrence of deceit, that he never uttered a falfhood himfelf, nor could pardon it in another. Cicero's letter to Lucceius, requefting him to write the hiftory of his life, "and "not to rejeƈt the generous partiality "of friendfhip, *but to give more to affec-* "*tion than to truth,*" is too well known to be recited here. *

But,

---

* In the intercourfe of friendfhip, the Romans do not appear to have difplayed much delicacy of fentiment. The paffages, which I have quoted from Cicero, evince the truth of this obfervation. Horace affords a further confirmation of it, in the clofe of his beautiful addrefs to Grofphus, Ode XVI. Lib. 2. And Pliny, in one of his familiar epiftles (Ep. XIX. Lib. 1.) difgraces an aƈt of the moft exalted generofity, by the infult to amity, which accompanies it. "Born," fays he to Romanus Firmus, "in the fame town, educated in the "fame fchool, and living together, from our early youth, in "habits of ftriƈt conneƈtion, I feel the ftrongeft motives to "promote the advancement of your fortune and dignity. I "fend

BUT, extravagantly as many of the
ancients have eftimated friendfhip, a modern writer, of diftinguifhed eminence,
has rated it ftill higher; and does not
hefitate to affert, that all the difcourfes
on the fubject, which are handed down
to us, appear to him flat and low, in
comparifon with the fenfe, which he en-
tertains of it. " This bond," he fays,
" diffolves every antecedent obligation,
" and the fecret, which I have fworn
" not to reveal to another, I may, with-
" out perjury, communicate to him, who

" fend you, therefore, three hundred thoufand fefterces,
" (£2421 fterling) to elevate you from the rank of Decurio,
" to that of a Roman Knight." But he then adds, " From
" my knowledge of your character, it is unneceffary to ad-
" monifh you to behave, in your new ftation, thus conferred by
" me, with the modefty, which becomes my beneficiary.
" For that honour fhould be folicitoufly preferved, in which
" the reputation of a benefactor is involved." *Ego ne illud
quidem admoneo, quod admonere deberem, nifi te fcirem fponte factu-
rum, ut dignitate à me data quam modeftiffime, ut a me data, utare.
Nam folicitius cuftodiendus eft honor, in quo etiam beneficium amici
tuendum eft.

" is

" is not *another*, but *myself*."* If the
author of the *Internal Evidence of Christianity*† had confined himself to such un-
warrantable ideas of friendship, when he
divefts it of the fanction of our divine
Law-giver, there could be no difficulty
in acquiefcing in his decifion. But an
affection, fo congenial to the principles
of our religion, when properly governed,
and judicioufly directed, feems to merit,
and, I truft, is not deftitute of, evangelical fupport. Benevolence is, indeed,
the great law of the Gofpel difpenfation;
but it muft have its commencement in
the more confined and partial charities:
And the man, who has felt not the appropriated regard of a fon, a brother,
a hufband, or a friend, cannot have a
heart capable of being expanded with
philanthropy. Even piety itfelf originates from the filial relation, and we learn
to transfer, to the Deity, that gratitude

* See Montaigne's Effays, Book I. Chap. 27.

† Soame Jenyns, Efq.

and

and veneration, with which the tender offices, and wifdom of our parents firſt infpired us. It is not the objeᏣt of Chriſtianity to overturn, but to regulate the œconomy of the human mind: And, if benevolence muſt have its foundation in private affeᏣtion, the divine law, which direᏣts the former, neceſſarily inculcates the latter.

That our Saviour himfelf experienced the tendereſt fympathies of friendſhip, may, I think, be juſtly deduced, both from his ſtrong attachment to John, the favourite difciple, and from the expreſ-ſions of peculiar endearment, with which he performed the miracle of raiſing Lazarus from the dead. On this affeᏣt-ing occaſion, the Evangeliſt relates, that *Jeſus wept:* And ſo fenſible were the Jews of the anguiſh of his foul, that they cried out, *Behold how he loved him!* * And,

* John, Chapter xi. ver. 35, 36. See fome admirable re-fleᏣtions on this fubjeᏣt, in the notes to Mr. Melmoth's tranſlation of Lælius.

if

if Chrift gave fuch a decifive proof of
perfonal attachment and friendfhip, the
hiftory of the Gofpel no lefs clearly
evinces, that his difciples felt an affection of the fame tender and peculiar
kind, to their Divine Mafter.   In the
pathetic converfation, which paffed, previous to the fufferings and death of
Jefus, when he prophetically, but tenderly charged them with their future
defection, Peter, in the warmth of his
regard, replied, *though I fhould die with
thee, yet will I not deny thee.*   The bitter
repentance of this Apoftle, fubfequent to
the mifconduct, which his great Mafter
had predicted, affords a further difplay
of the force of his friendfhip.   And
Chrift himfelf, afterwards, honoured
him with the kindeft and moft explicit
acknowledgment of it.   *So, when they
had dined, Jefus faith to Simon Peter, Simon
fon of Jonas, loveft thou me, more than
thefe?   He faith unto him, Yea, Lord, thou
knoweft that I love thee.   He faith unto
him,*

*him, feed my lambs. He faith unto him again, the fecond time, Simon, fon of Jonas, loveft thou me? He faith unto him, Yea, Lord, thou knoweft that I love thee. He faith unto him, feed my fheep. He faith unto him, the third time, Simon, fon of Jonas, loveft thou me? Peter was grieved becaufe he faid unto him the third time, loveft thou me? And he faid unto him, Lord, thou knoweft all things; thou knoweft that I love thee. Jefus faith unto him, feed my fheep.**

In the interefting paffage, here recited, that lively, reciprocal, and peculiar regard, which conftitutes friendfhip, is not only recognifed, but appealed to, and authorifed, as a generous and animating principle of action. And, if the great Founder of our religion has no where exprefsly ordained it, as a duty, it is probably, becaufe this virtue is of *fpecial,* and not of *univerfal* obligation ;

* John, Chap. xxi. ver. 15, 16, 17.

depending

depending on particular relations, and contingent circumftances, which human power can feldom influence or command. It may be added, too, that the divine law prefuppofes the exiftence of fuch affections, as are purely natural and fpontaneous; and directs its precepts, not to their production, but folely to their government and regulation. Hence, we find not, in the whole compafs of the fcriptures, one explicit injunction to parents, to love their children.* Yet, furely, this very effential moral office is not to be excluded from the catalogue of evangelical graces, notwithftanding the filence of facred writ, concerning it. And the fame plea may be extended to friendfhip, with due allowance for its rarer occurrence, and more partial obligation. The Chriftian, therefore, in perfect confiftency with his

* See Dr. Ogden's fermon on the duty of parents to children, Vol. II. p. 157.

faith,

faith, may admire and imitate the examples of generous amity, which hiſtory and obſervation exhibit to his view. *Peradventure for a good man*, ſays the Apoſtle, *ſome might even dare to die.* And the ſacrifice of our own eaſe, intereſt, or life itſelf, for the advantage of another, with whom we are connected by ſtrong and peculiar ties, may not only be juſtifiable, but highly honourable and meritorious. Let it be remembered, however, that the privileges of friendſhip are ſubordinate to the rights of ſociety; and that no attachment, merely perſonal, can warrant the violation of juſtice, fidelity, or truth.*

V. DISPU-

---

* The ideas, which have been entertained of VALOUR, and the LOVE of our COUNTRY, are ſtill more licentious than thoſe above recited, concerning FRIENDSHIP. It ſhould ſeem, that the underſtanding is dazzled by the ſplendour, which uſually accompanies theſe virtues; and that they are eſtimated by the rarity of their occurrence, or by the elevated ſtation of their poſſeſſors, rather than by the ſtandard of intrinſic merit, or public utility. Juſtice and probity are ſlightly regarded,

---

‘ V. DISPUTATION. *

POLEMIC SKILL is a dangerous
qualification; and, if not governed
by charity, wifdom, and integrity, may
betray the poffeffor, either into intemperate zeal, or abfolute indifference for
truth. Every object affumes an import-

as the *ordinary* duties of focial life, equally incumbent on all
ranks of men : And he, who practifes them, appears to have
no claim to more than common approbation. But great
exertions of courage or patriotifm, as they exceed the de-
mands, fo they proportionably excite the admiration of our
fellow-citizens. This admiration kindles in the mind an
enthufiafm, which often fufpends, and fometimes fuppreffes
the calmer principles of humanity, equity, and truth. And
the hero or patriot is indulged in all the privileges, which he
affumes; nothing being judged criminal, that promotes the
perfonal glory of the one, or the ambitious views of the other.
The hiftory of all ages confirms the truth of thefe obfervations :
But they are more particularly applicable to the records of
antiquity; which, for the moft part, celebrate the deeds of
warriors and ftatefmen, with unqualified applaufe, and without the leaft difcrimination of right and wrong.

* See page 102.

ance,

ance, in our eftimation, proportioned, in fome degree, to the labour and attention which we beftow upon it. And the fame enthufiafm, that dignifies a butterfly or a medal to the virtuofo and the antiquary, may convert controverfy into quixotifm; and prefent, to the deluded imagination of the theological knight-errant, a barber's bafon, as Mambrino's helmet.* The real value of any doctrine can only be determined, by its influence on the conduct of man, with refpect to himfelf, to his fellow-creatures, or to God. And it has been well obferved, by a writer, of diftinguifhed abilities, that fome kinds of error and fuperftition are fo intimately connected with truth and virtue, as to render the feparation of them impracticable, without doing violence to both. It is better, therefore, according to our Saviour's excellent advice,

* See Don Quixote.

to let a few tares grow up with the wheat, (if they be of such a nature, as to suffer the wheat to grow along with them,) than to endanger the destruction of the wheat, by rooting up the tares.*

Bigotry may be associated with truth, as well as with error: And this temper of mind is always unfavourable to piety and philanthropy, whatever be the principles on which it is founded. Erasmus asserts, that most of the reformers, with whom he was acquainted, became worse men, in consequence of the revolution, which they accomplished. I know not whether this fact will be admitted, on his authority. But certain it is, that the fury of zeal, and the acrimony of disputation, are neither consonant to the religion of nature, nor to the meek and peaceable spirit of the Gospel.

* See Priestley on the Sacrament, page 64.

But

But polemic fkill is fometimes employed in the defence of opinions, which
are known or believed to be falfe.
And, by this practice, the underftanding
either becomes the dupe of its own im-
pofitions; or acquires that indifference
to truth, which conftitutes incurable
fcepticifm, and fometimes terminates in
the moft fatal depravity. For he, who
has learned to be regardlefs of right and
wrong, in fentiment or in principle, can
have no folicitude about the like diftinctions, in his difpofitions or behaviour.
Such moral apathy gives full fcope to
every irregular defire, and vicious propenfity. And, if it be affociated with
great intellectual endowments, a character
may be formed, at once the glory and
the difgrace of human nature. Salluft
defcribes Catiline as *fubdolus, varius, cu-
juflibet rei* SIMULATOR *ac* DISSIMULATOR.
And I am inclined to believe, that the
remarkable portrait of SERVIN, which
the duke of Sully has drawn, owes fome

Y 3

of

of its moſt diſtinguiſhing features to the caufe, here alluded to. " Let the reader " reprefent, to himfelf, a man of a genius " fo lively, and an underſtanding ſo ex- " tenfive, as rendered him fcarcely igno- " rant of any thing that could be known; " of ſo vaſt and ready a comprehenſion, " that he immediately made himfelf " maſter of whatever he attempted; and " of ſo prodigious a memory, that he " never forgot what he had once learned. " He poſſeſſed all parts of philoſophy " and the mathematics, particularly for- " tification and drawing. *Even, in Theo-* " *logy, he was ſo well ſkilled, that he was* " *an excellent preacher, whenever he had a* " *mind to exert that talent, and an able* " *diſputant, for and againſt the reformed re-* " *ligion indifferently.* He not only under- " ſtood Greek, Hebrew, and all the " languages, which we call learned, but " alſo all the different jargons, or modern " dialects. He alſo accented and pro- " nounced them ſo naturally, and ſo

" perfectly

" perfectly imitated the gestures and
" manners, both of the several nations of
" Europe, and the particular provinces
" of France, that he might have been
" taken for a native of all, or any of
" these countries; and this quality he
" applied to counterfeit all sorts of per-
" sons, wherein he succeeded wonder-
" fully. He was, moreover, the best
" comedian and greatest droll, that, per-
" haps, ever appeared. He had a genius
" for poetry, and had written many
" verses. He played upon almost all
" instruments, was a perfect master of
" music, and sung most agreeably and
" justly. *He likewise could say mass; for*
" *he was of a disposition to do, as well as*
" *to know, all things.* His body was per-
" fectly well suited to his mind; he was
" light, nimble, dextrous, and fit for all
" exercises: He could ride well; and in
" dancing, wrestling, and leaping, he was
" admired. There are not any recre-
" ative games that he did not know;

Y 4

" and

" and he was ſkilled in almoſt all me-
" chanic arts.　But, now for the reverſe
" of the medal : Here it appeared, that
" he was treacherous, cruel, cowardly,
" deceitful; a liar, a cheat, a drunkard,
" and a glutton; a ſharper in play, im-
" merſed in every ſpecies of vice, a
" blaſphemer, an atheiſt.　In a word,
" in him might be found all the vices
" contrary to nature, honour, religion,
" and ſociety; the truth of which he
" himſelf evinced with his lateſt breath;
" for he died, in the flower of his age,
" in a common brothel, perfectly cor-
" rupted by his debaucheries, and ex-
" pired, with a glaſs in his hand, curſing
" and denying GOD."*

* See the Tranſlation of Sully's Memoirs, Vol. III. p. 92.

VI. INDIS-

VI. INDISCRIMINATE PLEADINGS OF LAWYERS.*

THE Roman orators undertook the defence of their clients, or dependents, in the courts of judicature, without fee or reward. And, under such circumstances, it might be supposed, that their pleadings would be regulated by the purest principles of justice or rectitude. But the fact was, frequently, far otherwise. Hortensius supported the cause of the infamous Verres: And even Cicero seems to have formed a design of undertaking that of Catiline, when he was brought to a trial, on account of his cruel and scandalous oppressions in Africa. For, in a letter to Atticus, he says, " It is my present intention to

* See page 108.

" defend

" defend Catiline. We have judges to
" our mind; yet such as please the
" accuser himself. I hope, if he be ac-
" quitted, it will incline him to serve
" me in our common petition."

Modern lawyers, in their ordinary practice, are governed by other motives, than those of ambition, or the desire of influence. Yet the profession, in its original establishment, appears to have disclaimed all mercenary considerations. And, even according to the laws, which now subsist, no counsellor can maintain an action for his fees, or so much as demand them, without doing wrong to his reputation.* He is liable, also, to a year's imprisonment, and to be condemned to perpetual silence, in the courts, if detected in the practice of deceit or collusion.†

* See Blackstone's Commentaries, Book III. Chap. 3.

† Statute Westm. I. 3 Edw. I. Chap. 28. Blackstone's Commentaries, Book III. Chap. 3.

How

How far the gentlemen of the bar have conformed themfelves to this ftatute, I am not competent to determine. But Bifhop Burnet relates, of the father of Sir Matthew Hale, that he had fuch ftrictnefs of confcience, as to lay down his profeffion, becaufe he difapproved of the common mode of *giving colour, in pleadings*; which he thought a culpable deviation from truth. It is recorded alfo of Sir Matthew Hale himfelf, that, whenever he was convinced of the injuftice of any caufe, he would engage no farther in it, than to explain, to his client, the grounds of that conviction. His biographer fays, that he abhorred the practice of mifreciting evidences, quoting precedents or books falfely or unfairly, fo as to deceive ignorant juries, or inattentive judges; and that he adhered to the fame fcrupulous fincerity in his pleadings, which he obferved in the other tranfactions of his life. For, he ufed to fay,

"it

" it was as great a difhonour, as a man
" was capable of, that, for a little money,
" he was to be hired to fay or do, other-
" wife than he thought." *

* See Britifh Biography, Vol. V. p. 383.

INDEX.

INDEX.

BACON,

INDEX.

B.

BACON, Lord, ftory of, 66.

BARBAULD, Mrs. her defcription of the night, 242.

Beauty, phyfical and moral, their relation to each other, 204.

BECCARIA, Marquis de, on the certainty of punifhment, 21.

BLACKSTONE, on the laws relative to duelling, 297.

BLOSSIUS, fact concerning, 308.

BOYLE, Mr. his piety and modefty, 114. His whimfical conceits in fome of his theological writings, 155.

BROWN, Mr. SIMON, curious account of, 127.

C.

CARNEADES, ftory of, 106.

CATO, the younger, cenfured, 302.

CHESTERFIELD, Lord, on the prudent concealment of truth, 38.

CHIAN-FU, ftory of, 32.

CHILO, curious fact concerning, 311.

CICERO, his folitary refidence at Aftura, 190. His loofe maxims concerning friendfhip, 311. Influenced his conduct on feveral occafions, 313. Seems to have intended to fupport the caufe of Catiline, 329.

Civility, forms of, confidered, 59.

Cock, curious account of one, 257.

COLUMBUS, ftratagem of, 24.

Counfel and *Reproof* difcuffed, 69, 70.

Courtefy, 62.

Crocodile, improperly defcribed by Dr. Young, 226.

CROMWELL, OLIVER, ftory of, 88. His conduct difcuffed, 90, 91, 92.

Curvilinear direction, in the motion of animals, 263.

D.

DIOGENES, ftory of, 65.

Difputation, 322.

T H E   E N D.